"Just re
Caiti coaxed

She pressed the shutter release. "Honestly, Griff, the pictures I've taken so far might do for a wanted poster, not a studio portrait. You could try smiling."

"Maybe what I need is incentive." Griff's smile was as intimate as a touch. "We could trade . . . kisses for photographs."

Caiti knew she ought to dismiss his suggestion, but his words stirred a fire deep within her. She forced a lighter note into her voice. "All right. But I'll set the terms. Three acceptable photographs—in advance."

"Three pictures for three kisses," Griff agreed.

Focusing quickly, Caiti captured the first shot. "That's one," Griff said, his voice heavy with anticipation. The shutter clicked again. "Two . . ." The shutter clicked a third time. "That makes three. Is it my turn now?"

Caiti nodded, unwilling to trust her voice as Griff slowly stood and came toward her. His words were a silky parody of her own. "Just relax, Caiti. . . . Just relax."

Julie Meyers is definitely an author to watch. She won the Romance Writers of America's Golden Heart Award for *Face to Face*, her first romance novel. She's since published one young adult novel, and she has a Harlequin Superromance scheduled for 1990. Julie is thrilled by these recent successes and is hard at work on future projects. A native of Michigan, Julie now lives in Northern California with her husband of fourteen years, her year-old daughter and three cats.

Face to Face
JULIE MEYERS

Harlequin Books

TORONTO • NEW YORK • LONDON
AMSTERDAM • PARIS • SYDNEY • HAMBURG
STOCKHOLM • ATHENS • TOKYO • MILAN

For my critique groups,
who never lost faith in Griff,

and for RDW, painter *extraordinaire*
and friend of the heart.

Published July 1989

ISBN 0-373-25358-3

1

SWALLOWING AGAINST the nervous knot in her throat, Caiti rang the doorbell again. Eight a.m., Nana had decreed, and 8:00 a.m. it was. So where was the elusive Griffon Falconer?

Romeo, Heathcliffe, Cyrano... In his three years as narrator and male lead for the "Heroes & Heartbreakers" radio broadcasts, Griffon Falconer had brought those and a dozen other roles to life with a romantic fervor that attracted thousands of new subscribers to FineArts Radio and extended its web of affiliate stations out from New York to encompass most of the major cities in the country. And as the audience multiplied, Griffon Falconer's personal popularity had risen, too, reaching the level of a genteel cult following.

"If we had that kind of name recognition working for us," Caiti had sighed two months ago, "this fund-raiser would run itself." And her fairy godmother, cleverly disguised as an elderly, white-haired volunteer named Marion Billinger—affectionately known as Nana—had replied, "Are you serious, dear? Griffon's my grandson. I'm sure he'd be glad to take part, if you really think it would help. Let me give him a call...."

Now, with eight long weeks of planning behind them, it was time to set the final wheels in motion. In a week's time, through the magic of advertising, Griffon Falconer's popularity was going to become a source of riches for

Caiti's favorite charity—assuming Mr. Golden-Throat Falconer ever deigned to answer his front door.

Hoping for the best, Caiti turned up the collar of her raincoat against the raw San Francisco morning and used the brass door knocker.

Throughout the first season of "Heroes & Heartbreakers," Griffon Falconer's photograph had been conspicuously absent from the monthly FineArts Radio programming guide. The omission had, of course, only served to stoke the curiosity of Falconer's fans. What did he look like? Was he tall, dark and handsome, as his voice seemed to promise? Elegantly slender? What color were his eyes? Where did he live? And, oh, was he married?

Giving up on the knocker, Caiti rapped her knuckles against the ornately carved Victorian door.

By the start of the second season, public pressure ensured that Griffon Falconer's picture appeared in the FineArts guide, alongside those of his fellow broadcasters. In a reasonable world, that should have been the end of the matter.

Instead, the furor had redoubled. The long-awaited photo displayed a patrician nose and intelligent dark eyes, but the rest of his face was obscured by an aggressive beard and mustache and a head of curly hair that reached his jawline.

And every strand is going to be worth its weight in gold, Caiti promised herself.

"Looking for me?" asked a voice from the fog behind her.

Having heard it for three years of Sunday broadcasts, Katie found the caressing baritone of The Voice unmistakably familiar. Taking a deep breath, she turned to face him. "Good morning, Mr. Falconer. I'm Caitlin Kelly." When he looked blank, she elaborated, "Your grandmother said I should meet with you this morning to talk about the festival."

"Oh! Right!" He stopped on the porch step below her. Despite the one riser advantage, Caiti found herself looking up to meet his eyes, dark as bittersweet chocolate. "Nana said someone would be coming, but I guess I was expecting a silver-haired society matron, not—"

Caiti felt a blush rising in her cheeks and tried to quell it, wishing for the millionth time that she weren't five foot two and freckled. Lifting her chin, she said, "I assure you, I'm old enough to drink, vote and drive, Mr. Falconer."

"Not all at the same time, I hope."

In spite of herself, Caiti smiled. "No. Not all at the same time."

"That's a relief. Seriously, though, I only meant that I was expecting someone closer to Nana's age than to mine. As surprises go, you're a very pleasant one, Ms Kelly."

Embarrassed, Caiti said, "Sorry if I sounded defensive."

"Sorry if I didn't make myself clear." He held out his hand to her. "And I'm sorry you had to wait. I did hurry."

Above the infamous beard, his cheeks were flushed, and the jacket of his gray jogging suit rose and fell as he tried to catch his breath. His fingers, grasping hers, were warm, despite the February morning's damp chill.

"Don't tell Nana I was late," he requested with a shamefaced grin, pulling a ring of keys from his jacket pocket. "She's a stickler for punctuality." When he had unlocked the door, he invited her inside.

As Caiti stepped into the dim foyer, a flicker of movement caught her eye. Turning, she found herself facing her own reflection in a massive antique mirror. Entranced, she reached to trace the leaf-and-vine carving of the frame with a careful fingertip. "Beautiful!"

"Yes," Griff agreed. "Beautiful."

Caiti froze as his hands came down to rest lightly on her shoulders.

"May I take your coat?" he asked mildly.

"Oh. Yes. Of course." Her fingers skittered over the buttons. "Thank you."

She regarded her reflection unhappily while Griffon crossed the foyer to hang her damp coat on the hall tree. An hour ago, her plaid wool skirt and navy pullover had seemed like cozy antidotes to a drizzly morning. Why did they suddenly look more like a fourth-grader's school uniform?

"You know," Griffon said over his shoulder, "I think we have something in common."

He was born sounding like that, Caiti told herself firmly. *It doesn't mean a thing.* "What?" she asked hoarsely, watching in the mirror as he came to rejoin her.

"Look at your hair."

"My hair?" Caiti repeated blankly. He was close behind her now. The top of her head fitted neatly beneath his chin. The warmth of him almost caressed her spine. When she tried to picture Nana and this magnetic stranger discussing her, her imagination balked. "What about my hair?"

He bent to bring his head level with hers. "It's exactly the color of mine."

With an effort, Caiti found her voice. "Yours is a halftone darker," she asserted. She had no prayer of understanding what made Griffon Falconer tick, but she understood color values; they were an integral part of her business.

"A halftone darker? Is it really?" Griffon's beard tickled against her cheek as he studied their paired reflections. "Could just be the lighting. What do you think?"

I think I was safer when you were just a voice on my radio, Caiti reflected ruefully. "Actually, Mr. Falconer—"

"Griff."

"Griff," she said, against her better judgment. "I don't mean to rush you, but—"

"But . . . ?" Griff prompted softly.

At such close range, The Voice was mesmerizing. Caiti groped for her train of thought. "But..." His mustache was rust, flecked with auburn; his beard was auburn, flecked with rust. His lips . . . Caiti took a drowning breath. "But I have to be at work by nine o'clock and it's already eight-fifteen, and I did want to discuss the plans for the fund-raiser with you before I go."

"The fund-raiser." Straightening, Griff took a deep breath of his own. "Right."

"I'm sorry to be in such a hurry, but—"

He looked repentant. "No, *I'm* sorry. I just got back last night from vacation. It always takes me a few days to remember that deadlines exist—my own or anyone else's. Forgive me?"

"Of course," Caiti assured him, and realized that she meant it. Forgiving him would be easy. Resisting him was going to be the hard part.

"In that case, let's go upstairs to the study." Griff crooked his elbow. "If m'lady will do me the honor?"

Already she knew it would be wiser not to touch him. And yet... *He's only being polite*, she chided herself. *And there's no point in offending him, not when he's being such a good sport about the Great Unveiling.*

"I feel as if I should have worn my crinolines," she said, slipping her hand into the bend of his arm. "Are we entering a time warp?"

"Not at all," he said, guiding her up the stairs. "But the world's a rough-and-tumble place. If a little courtesy can smooth our way, where's the harm?"

At the top, he led her to the nearest door and turned its crystal knob. "Please excuse the mess," he said, pushing the door wide.

It was a room from another age. Bookshelves lined the walls, reaching from the polished hardwood floor to the high ceiling. Persian carpets covered the space between a desk of carved mahogany and an elderly leather couch. Against the far wall, a fireplace nearly as tall as Caiti held a roaring blaze.

"What mess am I supposed to be excusing?" she asked, surveying the room with delight.

Griff gestured toward the slithering mountain of envelopes and magazines littering the desktop. "My mail. I had it forwarded from New York." He lifted an envelope that had slipped to the floor and added it to the pile. "That's the trouble with vacations. Leave town for three weeks and it takes three more just to catch up."

"Where did you go?" Caiti asked, watching as he bent to add a new log to the fire.

Griff dusted the wood bark from his hands. "Kauai."

"Kauai," she echoed, an envious shiver tracing down her spine. "It must have been blissful."

"A lovers' paradise," Griff said in a dry tone that belied his claim.

Shaking off a shiver of another sort, Caiti cursed her foolish preconceptions. Walking to the window, she looked out at the gray morning, where the fog was turning to rain.

Over the past three years, Griffon Falconer had become, for her, the embodiment of romance, a reliable source of comfort in the face of life's cruel unpredictability. Each Sunday, alone in the darkroom, hidden away from Papa Tony's gentle teasing, Caiti surrendered herself to The Voice, letting its smoky silk wrap her in another time, another place, where all the endings were happy and love was the one true touchstone.

She wanted to believe in that touchstone. If only for one hour a week, she needed the beautiful fantasies Griffon Falconer could spin. And, she realized belatedly, something in her had wanted to believe that he believed in that world of love and romance, without reservation or cynicism.

She never should have come.

No, that wasn't true. The reason for this meeting was the fund-raiser and all the people it would help, not some silly private daydream. If the price of guaranteeing Griff's participation was the discovery that her silver-tongued hero had a soul of clay, it was still well worth the cost.

"Didn't you have a good time there?" she asked, her curiosity piqued by his lack of enthusiasm.

"Not particularly. But I'm sure you didn't come here this morning to talk about my vacation."

Obeying the tacit No Trespassing sign, Caiti forced her attention back to the business at hand. "No, of course not. I'm sorry. When Nana arranged for us to meet today, I didn't realize you'd be on your way back from vacation. I thought you were coming to San Francisco on business."

"Only incidentally. Mostly I came to see Nana, and she suggested I meet with you." He smiled. "In my book, a suggestion from Nana outranks an order from anyone else, so here I am. Besides, I don't like to do things halfway. If I'm going to take part in this little money-maker of yours, I want time to rehearse."

It sounded like conventional English. Taken at face value, the words even made sense. In context, however,

Caiti found the notion ridiculous. "Rehearse?" she echoed, hoping she'd misheard him.

"Yes, rehearse. You know, practice. For the fund-raiser."

"But—"

"It's only a week away, so we don't have any time to waste. Nana said—" Griff's words stopped, and Caiti saw a hot flood of color stain his cheeks, overwhelming the more delicate flush left by his morning jog. "Damn," he said in a more subdued voice. "You don't know what I'm talking about."

"I'm afraid not," Caiti admitted.

Griff shook his head. "Looks like pride still goeth before a fall. When Nana said you wanted my help with your fund-raiser, I thought—I assumed—that you wanted me to perform." He managed a wry smile. "Well, no matter. They also serve who only stand and pay." Going to the desk, he opened the top drawer and produced a checkbook. "Did you have any particular amount in mind?"

Appalled, Caiti shook her head.

"Just asking. Don't look so stricken." Griff raised an agile eyebrow. "The cunning ones always leave it up to my sense of civic duty."

He was teasing, Caiti assured herself. He had to be. He couldn't really believe she expected a donation from him.

"Not even a hint?" Griff lowered his pen to the paper. "Well, then, how about . . ."

"No, please!"

He looked up at her in surprise. "Why so vehement, fair maiden? Don't you believe I have a sense of civic duty?"

"Of course you do. But so do we."

"We?"

"The fund-raising committee. We don't want your money. Not that there's anything wrong with your money," she added hurriedly, seeing the look on his face.

How had she blundered into this jungle of confusion? "But you're doing so much for us, it wouldn't be fair to expect a donation, too."

Griff sank into the desk chair, eyeing her with sudden misgiving. "Let me get this straight. You aren't here for a donation."

"No, of course not."

"And you don't want me to do a reading."

"No," she said, then amended, "unless you really want to, of course. It would be wonderful, but nobody's expecting you to, not on top of—"

"Everything I'm doing already," he supplied.

Caiti beamed in relief. "Exactly."

Griff leaned back in his chair. "I'm going to be sorry I asked this," he told the ceiling mournfully. "I'm going to ask, and she's going to tell me, and then I'm going to be sorry I asked." He smiled a martyr's gentle smile. "Have a seat, Ms Kelly."

She did as he asked.

"Now, tell me—preferably in words of one syllable— what is it, exactly, that I've agreed to do?"

Caiti tried not to stare. Maybe his vacation had been a rest cure, designed to restore an overtaxed mind. Maybe he was a victim of multiple personalities. Or blackouts. Or maybe, if she was very lucky, this was just his idea of a game, designed to attract her attention. If so, it was a rousing success.

"Mr. Falconer—"

He held up a warning finger.

"Griff," she corrected herself. "And you can call me Caitlin—or Caiti, if you'd rather." She smiled her best smile. "Be honest, Griff—you're teasing me, aren't you?"

"Now you're stealing my lines." He pushed up out of his chair and came to sit beside her on the couch. Taking both her hands in his, he said earnestly, "No need to make a mystery out of it. Just tell me what I'm supposed to do at your fund-raiser."

"But it was your idea!" she protested.

"Nevertheless, indulge me."

Caiti opened her mouth, willing to try, but the absurdity of the situation made her laugh instead. "You're not making this any easier," she scolded, "sitting there with that long face, like you're waiting for me to pronounce your doom."

"Never mind my face. Just begin at the beginning. I can take it. You say you're organizing a fund-raiser. Raising funds for what?"

"The Neighborhood." When he looked blank she explained, "It's a victim-assistance program. If your house is robbed or your store vandalized, or somebody mugs you and steals your wallet, you can call your local chapter of The Neighborhood and they'll come and do what they can to help."

"Pay for the damages, you mean?"

"Sometimes, if there's no insurance to cover it. But mostly we do immediate, practical things—help you nail plywood over the broken plate-glass window of your store, or sit with you in the Emergency Room until a doctor can stitch up the cut in your forehead, or just roll up our sleeves and help you clean up the mess. Whatever needs doing."

"Well, it sounds worthwhile," Griff conceded. "How long has The Neighborhood been around?"

"We're starting our fourth year. This will be the third annual fund-raiser."

"And how does this fund-raiser work?"

"We call it a festival. Each of the local chapters organizes a project—anything from a bake sale to a square dance. Sixty percent of the money they make from their project stays with the local chapter for work in their area, thirty percent goes into the master fund to finance major assistance projects, and ten percent gets reserved for publicity and membership drives."

"I see. So you're getting ready for this year's festival, and I'm supposed to help with *your* local chapter's project, right?"

Caiti sighed. It was easy to assume her familiar role as spokesman for The Neighborhood, but that didn't change the fact that Griff was still denying any memory of their plans just as tenaciously as he was holding on to her hands.

She tried to pull away.

"Right?" he persisted, retaining his grip. "Come on, you were doing just fine. Don't get stage fright now. The Neighborhood, the fund-raising festival, local chapters, sixty percent of the profits . . . for what? What am I supposed to do to earn you all that money? Hmm? Look at me."

Caiti tried to, but her gaze stayed riveted on the sight of his strong fingers entwined with hers, forming a lovers' knot. "Please let go," she entreated.

"Why? Are you leaving?"

Because I can't think when you hold my hands. No, she couldn't admit to the havoc he was wreaking on her blood pressure. "My nose itches," she said instead, and tried again to free her hands.

He leaned forward. "Where does it itch?"

Where did noses itch? "On the end," she said, and looked up to find Griff's face within inches of her own.

His eyelashes were the color of an Irish setter's coat. Under their luxuriant fringe, his eyes were a dense brown, so dark that it was hard to tell where the pupil ended and the iris began. Dark enough to lose her way in. . . .

"I'm going to sneeze," Caiti warned, alarmed by the intensity of that sable gaze.

"No you aren't." His words were a whisper of warmth against her skin. "Just hold your breath."

What breath? she wondered wildly, no longer able to guess what the next moment would hold, no longer able to do anything but watch as Griffon Falconer leaned closer still.

The tip of his nose touched hers. "There?" he asked.

"What?"

He turned his head slowly from side to side, brushing the end of his nose gently back and forth against hers. "Is this where it itches?"

He had skin like an English choirboy, pale and poreless, with a bright spot of color riding high on each cheekbone. Tiny laugh lines crinkled at the corners of his dark eyes. . . .

"Well, is it?" he asked.

"Is what?"

"Your nose," he said with elaborate patience. "Is this where it itches? Or are we just trading Eskimo kisses?"

"We—I—"

"Has your sneeze gone away?"

"Yes!" She drew a ragged breath. "Why are you doing this?"

"Doing what?"

Kissing me. The words danced in her mind, too dangerous to be spoken. "I thought we were going to talk about the fund-raiser," she said instead.

"I'm listening. I never stopped, actually. You just stopped talking."

"Well, I'm starting again!"

"And I'm listening."

"Then sit up straight and stop that. You're not an Eskimo."

"Ah. So now you think you know what I'm not," he challenged, straightening. "But do you know what I am?"

Caiti gathered her courage. "Well, for starters," she accused, not sure what his reaction would be, "you're an outrageous flirt."

Griff laughed, his face a picture of delighted surprise. "A hit. A palpable hit." He sobered slightly. "I'm sorry. There was no offense meant. But Nana said you wanted to meet the Griffon Falconer of 'Heroes & Heartbreakers,' and he's come to be known as a man of knowing glances and double entendres. Still, no matter. If you don't like him, we'll tell him to go away."

"And who will I find in his place?" Caiti asked, intrigued in spite of her better judgment.

"That depends. Who do you want me to be?"

"How about yourself?"

Griff shook his head decisively. "Not a good idea. He's no fun at all. Surely we can come up with a better idea than— Ah! I know!" Raising their joined hands briefly to his lips, Griff intoned " 'If I profane with my unworthiest hand/This holy shrine, the gentle fine is this:/My lips, two blushing pilgrims, ready stand/To smooth that rough touch with a tender kiss.' "

"That's lovely, but you're not Romeo."

"No?"

His expression reflected such wounded surprise, and then such rueful acceptance, that Caiti laughed. "I swear, Griffon Falconer, radio doesn't do you justice. You're a chameleon. You should be on the stage."

"Not a bad idea," he said, looking pleased. "Personally, though, I've never pictured Romeo in a full beard."

"True, but that won't matter, after next week."

His forehead furrowed. "What do you mean?"

"The fund-raiser."

"I don't see what the fund-raiser has to do with my future behind the footlights. Besides, I'm happy enough where I am...if we could just reach some agreement about who I ought to be. You've ruled out Romeo. Let me see who else I have on board." His expression changed again. With a sudden, ardent smile, he murmured, "'A kiss. The word is sweet/ What will the deed be? Are your lips afraid/ Even of its burning name?'"

Clutching at the rags of her composure, Caiti shook her head. "Cyrano you're not."

"You're right, of course. If I were Cyrano, I could have done my Eskimo kissing without ever getting up from the desk." His smile was full of mischief. "So. No Romeo, no Cyrano... I'm beginning to wish you weren't quite so well read."

"Maybe I'm just a good listener," Caiti parried. "If you only quote from old 'Heroes & Heartbreakers' episodes, it may just prove that I'm a devoted fan."

Griff's smile took on a dangerous new warmth.

"Of the show," Caiti qualified hastily.

He half closed his eyes, regarding her dreamily. "'They say the lady is fair—'"

"Griff—"

"'—'tis a truth,'" he reflected earnestly, "'I can bear them witness; and virtuous—'tis so, I cannot reprove it; and wise, but for loving me—by my troth, it is no addition to her wit, nor no great argument of her folly, for I will be horribly in love with her.'"

The crackling of the hearth fire was loud in Caiti's ears, and an answering warmth flamed in her cheeks. "Benedict's soliloquy," she managed to whisper. "*Much Ado About Nothing.*" Griff's eyes were closed, the fox-colored lashes lush against his skin. "Act Two." His hands still enfolded hers. "Scene Three."

The lashes stirred, and Caiti found herself impaled again on the dark strength of his gaze. "Full marks," he applauded softly. "And I believe you've proven my point. Definitely well-read." Another lazy blink. "Definitely fair—I trust the evidence of my own eyes. Definitely virtuous—as proved by your maiden blushes. But are you wise, Caitlin Kelly?"

There was no safe answer. In agitation, she searched for a question of her own. "Are you . . . ?"

"Am I what, Caiti-did?"

"Are you planning to be Benedict soon? For 'Heroes & Heartbreakers,' I mean?"

"I am already Benedict," he said with soft sincerity, and then smiled, dispelling the heady tension in the air. "For 'Heroes & Heartbreakers,' I mean," he mimicked gently. "It just hasn't aired yet."

"Oh."

"But it isn't general knowledge. FineArts hasn't released the new schedule yet."

"I won't—"

"I know you won't," he said, looking relaxed and friendly. "And if you did, it wouldn't really matter. The schedule is hardly a matter of national security. But I do think a fair trade is called for, don't you?"

"What do you mean? A fair trade of what?"

"I told you my secret—now you can tell me yours."

"Mine? But I don't have any secrets!"

He looked shocked. "What? No secrets at all?"

"None," she assured him.

He leaned back, eyeing her speculatively. "What about that wild summer you spent on the Riviera?"

"The Riviera?" Caiti laughed. "Now I *know* you're crazy. I've never even been to Reno, let alone the Riviera!"

"Hmm. My mistake. Well, then, what about that tiny birthmark behind your left knee that's an exact duplicate of the royal seal of Andorra?"

Caiti fought to keep her face straight. "Sorry, but no. I have freckles by the bushel, but no birthmarks, royal or otherwise."

Griffon sighed. "You're a hard case, lady, but I'm not giving up. Guard your secrets from me if you must . . . but answer me one question." Beneath his mustache, his grin widened rakishly. "What the hell am I scheduled to do at this crazy festival of yours?"

Caiti's heart pounded painfully in her chest. "You honestly don't remember?"

He placed his hand over his heart. "I honestly never knew to begin with. Enlighten me. Please."

"But Nana said—"

"Nana is an enchanting, endearing, exceedingly devious old woman whom you should trust roughly half as far as you can throw her. Break it to me gently, Caitlin. What has she done? What has she promised you that I'll do?"

He was serious. Caiti's heart sank.

"Caitlin?"

If The Neighborhood had acted in good faith, did their actions still constitute fraud? "Misappropriation of funds" had an ugly ring to it. . . .

"Talk to me, Caiti. Tell me what all this is about."

Caiti steeled herself. "The committee sent you a copy of the publicity flyer. It's probably on your desk. Read it. It explains . . . everything."

"I wish you'd quit looking as if I'd just shot your dog," Griffon scolded cheerfully. Going to the desk, he began sorting through the mound of mail. "I'm as good a sport as the next guy, you know. And while Nana may be devious, she's never malicious. I'm sure she just wanted to surprise me." He held an envelope aloft. "Is this it?"

Seeing The Neighborhood's familiar logo, Caiti nodded. Maybe he was right. Maybe it was just some sort of private joke between Nana and Griff. After all, Nana was one of The Neighborhood's staunchest supporters. Surely she wouldn't do anything to hurt it.

As Caiti watched, Griff slit the envelope and removed the colorful advertisement. He ran his gaze quickly down the printed page, then examined it again more slowly before lifting his shock-widened eyes to meet Caiti's hopeful look.

"You expect me to do *what?*"

2

"WELL, DON'T SHOOT the messenger," Caiti said. "It wasn't my idea."

"It certainly wasn't mine!"

She spread her hands placatingly, intimidated by his grim expression. "Don't look so horrified. Where's your sense of humor? It's hardly a fate worse than death."

"That's easy for you to say. Nobody's threatening to cut *your* beard off."

Picturing Griff's beard on her own small chin, Caiti fought to keep her face straight.

"This is serious!" Griff waved the brochure in agitation. "How many people have seen this thing?"

She searched her memory. "We sent out a first mailing of three hundred. But then FineArts got involved...."

"They would," Griff groaned. "The PR staff must have thought they'd died and gone to heaven. Who did you talk to?"

"A Mr. Sherwood, I think."

"Jack Sherwood. Damn. He probably laughed himself sick over it."

"He did seem to find it...entertaining," Caiti admitted.

"So," Griff said heavily, "what was the final body count? How many of these little gems actually hit the mail?"

She swallowed.

"How many, Caiti?"

"Ten thousand."

The bright flyer fell from Griff's grasp and fluttered to the carpet.

"I'm sorry, Mr. Falconer," Caiti said. "But be reasonable. You *did* give your okay for all this. You sent your grandmother a letter—"

His head jerked in tense rejection. "A postcard that said, in its entirety—and I quote—'Dear Nana, Glad to help out; fill me in when I get back from vacation. Love, Griff.' It's obvious, now, that I should have called her and gotten all the details, but I thought it would be okay, whatever it was. I wouldn't have cared if it was something silly, or time-consuming, or..." Pacing back to the couch, he loomed over Caiti. "She never said anything to me, not *one word*, about having to shave my beard. The deal's off. I don't care if you've sent out ten million of these things. I won't do it. I won't!"

Stunned by his outburst, Caiti tried again to explain. "Mr. Falconer, we—"

"No." The imperious tone of The Voice cut her off. "Watch my lips, Ms Kelly. The answer is no. Absolutely, nonnegotiably no. I don't care what Nana promised you. I don't care how worthy a cause your Neighborhood is. I will *not* be bullied into shaving off my beard by you or Nana or anyone else."

In the ringing silence that followed his words, Caiti's anger and embarrassment battled to a draw, leaving her numb. "It was never our intention to bully you into anything," she said quietly, and stood up. "Believe me, I'm sorry about this misunderstanding, for your sake and ours. Thank you for your time."

He stared at her, the anger in his eyes giving way to confusion. "But—"

"I've taken up too much of your morning, to no good purpose. Goodbye, Mr. Falconer."

"Wait."

"I have to go now," Caiti said firmly, walking to the door. "I'm late for work."

"Five more minutes won't matter," he objected, pursuing her.

"What's the point?" She reached the polished banister. "Done is done," she said over her shoulder, starting down the stairs.

"Ms Kelly—" He drew even with her. "Caitlin—" Reaching the bottom step, Griff slipped past her, blocking the path to the front door. "Wait a minute, would you?"

"Why?" Caiti demanded, perplexed and distressed. "I'm going to go away and leave you in peace. Isn't that what you told me to do? Isn't that what you want?"

"No. I mean, yes, but—"

Caiti waited.

"Look," he said, "I know it doesn't help, but I'm sorry I can't do what you ask."

"Are you?" She forced a smile, determined to escape before the numbness faded and the full import of the disaster could hit home. "If you didn't know about it, then it really isn't your fault. End of subject, all right?"

"Now you're the one who's mad," he observed.

"I'm not mad."

"You look mad."

"Well, I'm not." Seeing the disbelief in his eyes, she qualified, "Disappointed, maybe, and confused. But not mad. At least, not at you."

"Upset, then."

Her patience was wearing thin. "And what if I am? Don't I have a right to be?"

"So I'm keeping my beard," he said defensively. "Is that so terrible?"

Being a good sport was one thing. Lying through her teeth for the sake of Griff Falconer's peace of mind was quite another. "Yes," she snapped, "as a matter of fact, it is terrible, at least from my point of view! I know you'd feel better about all this if The Neighborhood turned out to be a bunch of loonies and dreamers, but it isn't."

Griff cocked an eyebrow. "Oh, come on. Your group may not be loony, but the idea certainly was. Be realistic! How could you expect to make any money from having me shave my beard?"

"If you'll quit looking so skeptical for two seconds, I'll tell you how," Caiti burst out, stung by the implication that the fund-raiser might have failed even with his cooperation. "We sold tickets for people to come and watch the demise of your precious beard. We called it 'The Great Unveiling.' We talked the most exclusive men's hair stylist in town into doing it, free of charge, and—"

Griff looked relieved. "If that's all, I don't think my conscience will keep me awake too many nights. You must have had the Devil's own time getting people to pay good money to watch some radio jerk being given a shave and a haircut."

"The Devil's own time?" She lifted her chin stubbornly. "I guess that depends on your definition. The original fifty tickets sold out in less than a day. By the time FineArts approached us, we'd already changed the location to the school auditorium. It seats six hundred and we've sold out, down to standing room."

"All right." Griff held up his hand in surrender, then ran it self-consciously over his beard. "I give up. Fair is fair. I won't shave my beard off, but I'll make up for the money you're losing. Six hundred dollars." He rolled his eyes. "The most valuable beard in town."

"More valuable than you think," Caiti retorted. "Better check your facts before you start making magnanimous offers, Mr. Falconer. Those tickets sold for twenty dollars apiece."

"Twenty apiece? But that's twelve thousand dollars!"

"I know. Believe me, I know." She'd been so excited— they'd all been so excited—at the thought of the good that money was going to do. . . .

Griff leaned back against the front door as if he no longer trusted his knees. "Look, Ms Kelly, I'll be honest with you. I don't have twelve thousand dollars. Not in a lump sum I can hand you today. But I meant what I said about being fair." He swallowed. "Maybe we could work out some sort of payment schedule and . . ."

"Why should you, if you never agreed to the plan in the first place?" Absurdly, she was beginning to feel sorry for Griffon Falconer. "Besides, twelve thousand dollars wouldn't begin to cover what we're going to lose. Not anymore."

"Why not?" he demanded, then shook his head. "No, don't tell me, let me guess. FineArts?"

"FineArts. I don't know how they heard about it, but they sent Mr. Sherwood out to talk to us, and he dreamed up a way to involve FineArts subscribers from all across the country."

"All across . . . ? Good grief, this thing's a nightmare. What was Jack going to do, videotape it?"

"Actually he said he wished he could, but FineArts hadn't lined up a television affiliate yet."

"Thank God for small favors," Griff said earnestly. "What did he have in mind, then? Even Jack isn't crazy enough to think the snick-snick of barber's shears would make a fascinating radio show, is he?"

"No," Caiti agreed, smiling wanly at Griff's theatrical dismay.

"Then what did he dream up?"

"Well, he claimed Waste Not, Want Not was the motto at FineArts—"

"True enough. Shoestring budgets have always been their speciality."

"So he suggested that we make the most of what we had. Actually what you had. Or, rather, what you used to have. That is, what you *would* used to have had, if we'd gone ahead the way we planned."

"Caiti, you're not making any sense. Simplify it for me. What did Jack want you to make the most of?"

Given Griff's earlier reaction, she was almost afraid to tell him. "The hair."

"What hair?"

"Your hair. The hair they planned to cut off."

Griff snorted. "What was he going to do, keep it in a FineArts scrapbook, like a baby's first tooth? I wouldn't have pegged Jack as a sentimentalist."

"No, it wasn't anything like that. He put a paragraph in last month's FineArts bulletin, explaining about our fund-raiser and offering to send a lock of your hair to any subscriber who made a donation to The Neighborhood."

"He *what*?"

"He put a paragraph in—"

"My hair?" Griff echoed in stark disbelief. "A lock of my hair? Are you serious?"

"I'm afraid so."

"But that's *sick*! What's the matter with him? Our listeners are intelligent people, not some mindless bunch of groupies. Jack knows that. Nobody in their right mind—"

"It wasn't like that," Caiti protested. "The paragraph Mr. Sherwood put in the FineArts bulletin was sort of . . . tongue-in-cheek. Humorous. He was inviting the subscribers to do something silly for a good cause, that's all."

"And how much was he charging them for the privilege of making fools of themselves?"

"He didn't name a price. He just explained what The Neighborhood was, and . . . and left it up to them."

If Griff had seemed pale before, he now looked ashen. "Wonderful. Any con man knows that's the best way to increase the take, if you've made a slick pitch." He rubbed his temples. "Okay, level with me. How many fell for it?"

Caiti's temper sparked again. "Nobody 'fell' for anything. The Neighborhood isn't some shady rip-off!"

"Excuse *me*," Griff said with acid formality. "Let me reword the question. May I ask just how many public-spirited FineArts listeners responded to Jack's little appeal and mailed in their tax-deductible donations, Ms Kelly?"

"At last count, about three thousand of them."

"*Three thousand?* And they each want a souvenir? You must be joking! At that rate, I'll look like Yul Brynner! I mean, I would, if I went through with this stunt, which I certainly don't intend to."

Caiti scowled. "You've made that abundantly clear. Not that it would have been a problem, anyway. As beautiful as your hair may be, Mr. Falconer, not everyone *wanted* a lock of it. Most of the people who sent in donations were just doing a kind, decent thing."

"Meaning that I'm refusing to do a kind, decent thing?"

"You said it, I didn't." Caiti took a firm hold on her temper. "Look, Mr. Falconer, I'll be honest with you. The Neighborhood is important to me, and so is this fundraiser. I'd be delighted if you changed your mind and decided to help us out. But I'll also be the first to admit that you've got a right to keep your beard, if it's that important to you."

"It is." He shook his head hopelessly. "It is. I wish I could explain, but . . ."

"You don't owe me any explanations."

Griff sighed and held out his hand. "Maybe not. But I like you. I'd like to know you better." His fingers closed gently over hers. "Believe it or not, I'd like you to think well of me. So tell me—how much did the FineArts contributions raise? Maybe we can still work something out."

It was Caiti's turn to sigh. "The average donation was ten dollars, but some people gave more."

Griff stared at her in fresh alarm. "But you said you had responses from three thousand subscribers. Are you telling me you raised—"

"Between the FineArts contributions and the ticket sales, we've raised over forty thousand dollars." She blinked back the tears that rose without warning to sting her eyes. "You can't expect me to smile happily while all that disappears. The Neighborhood had big plans for the money." She lifted her shoulders in an exhausted shrug. "Still, that's our problem, not yours."

Griff's thumb drew a restless pattern on the back of her hand. "God knows, I'm looking for a way not to be the villain in this. But if I couldn't hand you twelve thousand dollars, I certainly can't hand you forty thousand. And I just can't do what those flyers say I'm supposed to." He squeezed her hand apologetically. "I...can't explain. If we knew each other better, I might ask you to take me on faith. But to do that now would be pretty presumptuous." He pressed a soft kiss to the back of her hand. "I'm sorry. I know it doesn't help, but I am sorry."

"It wouldn't be forever," she whispered, hating herself for begging. For hoping. "Your beard would grow back...."

Silence. Griff released her hand. "I'm sorry," he repeated.

"So am I," Caiti said miserably, keeping her eyes on the polished hardwood planks beneath her feet.

Griff's sudden sigh was a warm gust of frustration. "Just wait till I get my hands on Nana. She knew exactly what she was doing when she set this whole thing up."

Caiti looked up at him, appalled. "I'm sure she had a reason."

"A reason?" Griff's answering laugh was harsh. "You can bet on it."

"No, I mean a good reason," Caiti persisted. "Nana's a wonderful lady. She cares about The Neighborhood. And she cares about you."

"Whatever her motives were, she tried to use you to manipulate me, and it makes me angry. You deserve better than that, Caiti." His fingertips traced the angle of her cheekbones. "Damn it, we both deserve better...."

Caiti closed her eyes as Griff pressed his lips to her eyelids, her forehead, the tip of her nose.

She ought to stop him. He was angry with her...wasn't he? And she had been angry with him, had been ...

Lost in the darkness, Caiti felt his fingers threading gently through her hair. *He's got an image to maintain*, she warned herself despairingly. *This is what heartbreakers are supposed to do.*

"Caitlin," he breathed, and lowered his mouth to hers.

She was braced to resist finesse, but Griff's kiss was an artless cry of need, and Caiti found herself flowering beneath it, sharply aware of the smooth caress of his lips, the tickle of his beard and mustache, the clean, warm taste of him.

He drew back slightly, cradling her face in his hands. "What is it about you?" he asked breathlessly. "I swear, I didn't mean to do that."

Caiti searched for her voice. "Is that an apology?"

"Only if you're . . . offended."

She shook her head in gentle denial.

"In that case, think of it—" a wisp of a smile played at the corner of his mouth "—as a promissory note. I don't pretend to have a forty-thousand-dollar kiss, but I'm damn well going to find a way out of this mess that will satisfy both of us." Reluctantly he released her. "I know you're late for work, but could we get together for dinner tonight, to talk about it? Where do you live? How can I—"

Behind them, a key rasped in the lock, and the front door swung open.

"Well, Griffon, here you are, home again—however briefly!" The young woman who swept into the foyer was blond and stylish, dressed in knee boots and a swirling coat of ivory wool. Furling her dripping umbrella, she said, "I hope you're happy with yourself, dragging me out on a morning like this."

Caiti watched as Griff's expression hardened. "And a gracious good morning to *you*. Don't you ever knock? Caiti, this is Denise, my—"

"Is Marion ready?" Denise interrupted, unbuttoning her coat.

"No. She was still asleep when I went out for my run."

"It's high time she was up." Denise paced to the foot of the stairway, her motions sharp with impatience. "I don't intend to make an all-day project out of this."

"Nobody's asking you to make any 'project' of it at all," Griff said testily. "Frankly I think it's a lousy idea. Why don't you just go back home and we'll forget the whole thing?"

"No."

"Well, there's no point in dragging her out of a warm bed and into a cold rainstorm. Why don't we wait, at least, and do it tomorrow?"

"Because tomorrow's Saturday and I have other plans," she snapped. "Honestly, Griffon, I don't know why I bother explaining myself to you. Marion wanted to wait until you got back from your trip, so I made the arrangements for today, and she agreed to them, and that's the end of the matter. You've got no business interfering."

"No business! You're a fine one to talk about—" Ruddy with anger, Griff stopped himself in midsentence. "This isn't the time or the place for a shouting match," he said stiffly. "Would you mind waiting for me upstairs, Denise?"

"Poor Griffon. Did I interrupt you at an awkward moment?"

Griff turned to Caiti. "I'm sorry. Could you wait for me here for a minute? Please?"

"Never mind," Denise said before Caiti could respond, "I'll get Marion myself." And she started up the stairs.

"Damn it, no!" Griff bounded after her. "I don't see why you're pushing so hard on this," he objected, The Voice giving a razor edge to his irritation.

"It's for Marion's own good, as you'd well know if you were ever here to shoulder your share of the responsibility instead of running off to live the bohemian life in New York—"

They vanished upstairs, their voices fading to silence.

Alone in the foyer, Caiti retrieved her coat with shaking hands. Who was that woman? Griff's words seemed to hang on the silent air: *"Caiti, this is Denise, my—"*

Your what? she wondered, and found, to her surprise, that she was afraid of the answer.

It was time to go. It was long past time to go. This was no place for her, not just because of Denise's intrusion or Griff's refusal to take part in the fund-raiser, but because of Griffon Falconer himself. In less than an hour, he had unraveled three years' worth of her self-control. Whatever voltage powered him, it was clearly too strong for her emotional wiring. His ability to intrigue and infuriate her ruled out the possibility of simple friendship, and any other relationship was far too dangerous even to contemplate.

Besides, if he was determined to keep his beard, there was no reason for her to cross his path again. Any further appeal on The Neighborhood's behalf would have to come from his grandmother.

The thought was a hot pain in Caiti's chest. *Why won't he help, Nana? You promised he would, and I believed you. We all believed you. What are we going to do now?*

Shivering, she pulled on her coat and stepped out into the rain.

IT TOOK GRIFF half an hour, not the "minute" he had so optimistically predicted, to talk Denise into going home. When the big front door finally closed behind her, he heaved a heart-felt sigh of relief.

Never, if he lived to be a hundred, would he learn to deal calmly with Denise. Living in New York the past few years, he'd managed to downplay the memory of her caustic tongue, but nothing had really changed: a word from her could still reduce him to defensive anger and an adolescent urge to do exactly the opposite of whatever she wanted.

It hadn't always been that way....

Griff flinched at the thought. Past was past. It was a mystery to him how anyone so beautiful could be so persistently ill-tempered.

"They say the lady is fair..." he quoted wryly, then froze in open-mouthed dismay as he remembered what Denise's grand entrance had interrupted.

"Caiti?"

His voice echoed in the empty foyer.

"Caitlin?"

But her raincoat was gone, and so, it seemed, was she.

Griff frowned. Of course she was gone. In less than an hour she'd been kept waiting, flirted with, teased, yelled at, kissed, insulted and deserted. After a performance like that, who in her right mind would wait around for an encore? She'd probably bolted as soon as his back was turned, breathing a fervent prayer that she'd seen the last of Griffon Falconer.

But he wasn't about to let that prayer be answered. He had to find her, see her, talk to her again—

Why? Why did he feel so urgent about a woman he barely knew? What was so special about Caitlin Kelly?

It wasn't a matter of falling for a pretty face. That was one mistake he was never likely to make. Objectively he knew that Caiti's green eyes and pale skin were a pleasing combination with the rich auburn of her chin-length curls; that the tilt of her short nose lent her face a certain gamine charm; that her smile revealed teeth that were small and white and even. Still, the overall effect was more wholesome than intoxicating.

Not that he was complaining. Physical beauty was an untrustworthy external, a lucky roll of the genetic dice, not a true indication of the person within. On the whole, spectacular good looks had proved to be a warning flag: here's someone to avoid.

But if Caiti's looks had failed to bowl him over, what had it been? Not her voice, certainly. As part of FineArts Radio, Griff lived and worked in a world of sound. High or low, bright or sultry, the human voice was an instrument to be played, a tool to be wielded with conscious skill to achieve a predetermined effect. Caiti's voice was pleasant, perhaps even melodious, but it was untrained and her use of it was transparently uncalculated. Granted, that very lack of calculation had its charm . . . but the attraction he felt was fueled by more than an honest voice.

All right, then, he'd ruled out the way she looked and the way she sounded. What, then, had roused him from his lethargy and pushed him beyond the idle word-play of flirtation? It couldn't be anything so insubstantial as the scent of her. As far as he could remember, she'd worn no perfume at all, smelling only of soap and herbal shampoo.

But the embrace that had brought him close enough for her subtle scent to reach him was another matter. He could still feel the scratchy wool of her sweater, the silk of her hair, the moist, trembling satin of her lips beneath his. . . .

Griff walked quickly to the foot of the stairs, shaken by the desire his thoughts rekindled.

What was the matter with him? He wasn't some sex-starved adolescent. Was this sudden fascination with Caitlin Kelly just a response to his solitary vacation and the emptiness of his New York life? Was he so hungry for a relationship that the first presentable woman to cross his path inevitably ignited him like dry tinder?

No. He suspected that what had really attracted him to Caiti, the difference that made her stand out from the other women he knew, was the gleam of commitment shining in her eyes when she talked about The Neighborhood. She seemed to care deeply—not just about the organization but about the people it was designed to help. She was doing something constructive, something useful, something unmistakably real.

He admired her for that, admired and envied her.

Three years ago, radio had seemed like a liberating arena, a wonderland where the pictures he painted with his voice could eclipse the limits of the physical world. Lately, though, that satisfying sense of magic had begun to pall.

When a growing sense of isolation began to undermine his confidence and affect his performances, he'd insisted on a vacation. Hoping it was just a case of midwinter doldrums, he'd traveled to the warm shores of Kauai and waited for the change of scene and climate to clear his mind and renew his enthusiasm.

But it hadn't. After three weeks of mental debate, he'd flown back last night, still depleted, still lonely, still undecided about renewing his contract with "Heroes & Heartbreakers." Was it time to move on? To make a change?

Isolation. The word crept back into his mind, persistent as a ghost. Troubled by it, Griff sat down on the steps. Was that sense of isolation the connecting thread? He'd assumed that his personal loneliness was a separate problem from his growing dissatisfaction at FineArts Radio. But what if it wasn't? What if his frustrations over the lack of a live audience and FineArt's continuing refusal to let him involve himself in the show's production were facets of the same loneliness he felt so keenly in his private life? Could he cure one without resolving the other?

"Heroes & Heartbreakers" had been good to him. Its popularity was still on the rise. The smart decision—the safe decision—would be to stay put and ride the wave for another season or two, while he weighed his options.

But staying with the show demanded a price. He was lucky if he got back home to California once a year, and he hadn't met anyone in New York who could fill the void in his life. He had plenty of acquaintances and a few real friends, but he had yet to find anyone special, anyone who could ease the hunger building within him.

His thoughts strayed back to Caiti. Why had she left? Where was she now? Gone to work, by her own account. He wondered what she did for a living. Something meaningful, probably, like her volunteer work with The Neighborhood. But what, exactly? And where?

He might not know where to find Caiti, but he knew where to find out—from Nana. In fact, he reflected, stroking his beard, Nana had a great deal more than that to answer for.

With fresh energy, he bounded up the stairs to the second floor, stopped outside the only closed door and knocked.

"Friend or foe?" a voice inside demanded.

"Foe," he said sternly.

"Go away, then. I'm asleep."

Fighting the amusement that welled up in him at her response, he knocked again.

"Friend or foe?" the question came again.

"Friend," he stated, and pushed the door open.

Sitting on the edge of her big brass bed in a flannel nightgown, Nana smiled disarmingly at him, her face

wreathed by strands of silver hair that had escaped from
her braids in the course of the night. "Good morning, dear.
Did you sleep well?"

Despite his frustration, Griff found himself returning
her smile. "Fine, thanks. My troubles didn't start until after I got up."

"Troubles?" Nana's eyes widened. "Is anything wrong?"

"Nothing you can't explain away, I'm sure." He crossed
his arms. "I've met your friend."

"My friend?"

"Caitlin Kelly. You do know her, I trust?"

Nana nodded. "Of course. A sweet girl."

"Yes. Well. Your 'sweet girl' and I had a little talk. About
my beard."

"Oh, dear," Nana said ingenuously.

"And now I need to know where to find her."

"Have you lost her?"

He wanted to yell at Nana, to shake her until she
dropped the game and told him what he wanted to know.
But something about the way she sat there, tugging nervously at her braids like a guilty child, crept beneath the
defense of his anger. "I swear," he said with helpless af-
fection, "with your hair like that you look about three
years old, not eighty-three."

"It keeps the snarls out while I sleep. Of course, Denise
says I should cut it all off—it would be so much more
practical." Nana's eyes glinted mischievously. "I heard her
tender dulcet tones in the hallway a little while ago. Has
she left yet or shall I indulge in another forty winks?"

"The coast is clear for now, you renegade."

"In that case, it's high time I was up." Levering herself
upright, Nana walked stiffly to the cherrywood vanity
table and lowered herself onto its stool by cautious degrees. "Poor Griffon," she said, her eyes meeting his in the

mirror's bright surface. "Denise must have been in rare
form to put such a frown on your face."

"Denise is the least of my worries, this morning—as you
know perfectly well. As long as we're on the subject,
though, why don't you just explain to her that you don't
want to go look at that retirement community?"

"'Retirement community'? Old folks' home, you mean."
Unbraiding her hair, Nana sighed. "As to why I let her
come...she wore me down. Denise is inexhaustible when
it comes to managing other people's affairs. Tease me if
you like, but I simply didn't have the energy to go on arguing with her about it." She lifted a silver-backed brush
from the vanity. "Perhaps I am getting old."

Griff's first impulse was to deny it with a laugh, but the
morning light fell uncompromisingly on Nana's wrinkled
face, and he saw that the past night's sleep had been powerless to erase the pale violet shadows beneath her eyes.

She wasn't indestructible, he admitted to himself. No
one lived forever. Crossing the floor to stand behind her,
he took the brush and ran it slowly through her hair. "I
shouldn't have kept you up so late last night talking."

"Nonsense," she objected spiritedly. "What's the use of
being an adult if I go to bed at eight every night? It's been
entirely too long since I burned the midnight oil. Besides,
I've missed our talks. I've missed you. These days, I'm just
a little slower getting started in the mornings, that's all. I'll
be ready for a tiger hunt by noon."

The vigor in her voice was heartening, but the arthritic
stiffness of her movements made Griff's conscience sting.
"It's for her own good," Denise had scolded, *"as you'd well
know if you were ever here to shoulder your share of the
responsibility."* Working in New York, had he given short
shrift to his responsibilities? If the time had come when it

was no longer wise for Nana to live alone, then it was his place to find a solution, not Denise's.

"I'll make sure the elephants are ready," he teased, but his heart was heavy. His love for Nana gave him certain rights—and certain responsibilities. In a childhood of endless boarding schools and new stepmothers, his only really happy times had been the summers he'd spent in this house with her. He'd lived in New York for seven years now, pushing ahead with his career, but no one there knew him or cared about him the way Nana did. No one else had her talent for seeing through his mask.

And when she died, and there was no one left to see him clearly, he would die a little, too.

"Such a sober face," Nana chided. "It's going to take more than one late night to send me off to meet my Maker."

She was right, of course; it was stupid to waste their time together moping because some day she'd be gone. Right now she was here, and very much alive.

"By the way," she continued airily, "I'd like you to drive me over to the theater to see Daniel this morning."

Three decades in her company had taught Griff the signs of mischief afoot. Whatever was prompting the suggestion, Nana's interest in it wasn't idle. "My pleasure," he said, matching her casual tone. "I'll drop you off and run some errands while the two of you visit."

"Well, actually, Griffon . . ."

He waited, watching as her reflected expression changed from innocence to candor.

"Actually," she admitted, "it's you he wants to see. I had lunch with him last week and told you you were coming home. There's something he wants to discuss with you."

"Ah. The plot thickens. I don't suppose your old friend Daniel mentioned what that 'something' was?"

Nana shrugged. "You know Daniel—he always has some new idea up his sleeve. Surely there's no harm in listening to what he has to say."

"This isn't a tiger hunt you're organizing," he protested with a laugh. "It's a visit to Daniel and the lion's den! If I had a brain in my head, I'd run the other way."

"But you're curious, so you'll come, won't you, Griff?"

"I'll come," he said, handing the hairbrush back to her. "But first you're going to tell me all about Caitlin Kelly."

AT THE BUONARROTI Photography Studio, Caiti worked through the rest of Friday in a haze. Through the lens of the camera, her eyes focused on the customers who posed at her instruction, but her thoughts stumbled endlessly from Nana to Griffon to the fund-raiser. After each sitting, she dialed Nana's phone number, but her calls rang unanswered.

As worried as she was, Caiti resisted the temptation to call the other members of the fund-raiser committee before she knew all the facts. Nana's granddaughter was scheduled for a portrait sitting on Saturday morning; Caiti would wait and get her answers then.

But her mind still gnawed at the problem. With the festival a week away, there was little hope of reorganizing the fund-raiser around a new theme. Even if they did, there was no guarantee it would catch the imagination of the public as surely as their original campaign. In all likelihood, the bulk of the money would have to be returned.

Forty thousand dollars. It was a lot of money to lose. And what about the damage to The Neighborhood's credibility? The new names on the mailing list and the companies that for the first time had felt moved to contribute would probably be lost to them, and some of their long-time supporters might abandon them, as well. . . .

But the worries that dogged her on Friday were less unsettling, in their way, than the memories that came that night to fill her mind as she drifted on the edge of sleep: memories of auburn and rust, rust and auburn, dark eyes and gentle hands and the singular beauty of The Voice. Memories of a soft, searching kiss, the first to touch her lips in three long years.

Sleep came at last, but with it came the dreams—hot, sweet fantasies that woke her again and again, aching and alone. She listened to the uneven patter of rain against her window, waiting for her pulse to slow so that sleep could reclaim her, but each return to her dreams found him waiting for her. At times, she could see him clearly, feel the warmth of his hands, taste the healing touch of his lips. But there were other dreams where he was invisible, intangible, and only The Voice caressed her, haunting her ears, vibrating against her skin, promising pleasure and adoration but leaving her empty and unfulfilled.

It was a relief to wake to the gray light of morning. Sitting up, Caiti found the sheet bunched at the foot of the bed and the soft folds of the blanket wrapped, cocoon-like, around her. Untangling herself from its embrace, she showered and dressed and went upstairs to Papa Tony's apartment, to fix breakfast for the two of them. Then, resolving to put Griffon Falconer out of her mind until she had talked to Nana, she went down to open the studio and face the day.

Facing the day, however, also meant facing Mrs. Ames. The portly bookkeeper was already waiting on the front step, umbrella in hand, when Caiti unlocked the door.

"So tell me," she demanded cheerfully as she crossed the threshold. "What was Griffon Falconer like?"

Caiti smiled wanly. "Good morning, Mrs. Ames. Papa Tony has a wedding in Berkeley this morning, and I've got

Mrs. Billinger's grandaughter coming in at nine-thirty. Would you mind listening for the phone while she's here?"

"No trouble," Mrs. Ames assured her, reanchoring her hairnet. "No trouble at all. Now tell me! What did you think of Griffon Falconer? For the love of heaven, talk to me, girl! I've been on tenterhooks all week. What was he like? Is that voice of his as dreamy in person as it sounds over the radio?"

Caiti turned the sign from Closed to Open. "You can rest easy, Mrs. Ames. The Voice is real, not some sound engineer's trick."

"How tall is he?"

The only way to deal with Mrs. Ames's appetite for detail was to satisfy it. Bracing herself, Caiti answered, "Tall. Six foot three or four, I'd guess."

"What color is his hair?"

"A half shade darker than mine," Caiti said, and swallowed an unexpected lump in her throat.

"Here, now, what's wrong? I thought he'd be wonderful. I thought you'd be floating!"

Caiti struggled to regain her smile. "He is. I was."

"But . . . ?"

"But he isn't going to do the fund-raiser."

Mrs. Ames bristled. "Why on earth not? What a nerve!"

"No, it isn't like that."

"Then what is it like?" Mrs. Ames demanded indignantly.

"He says he didn't know anything about it! Nana Billinger told us he'd agreed to everything, but . . ."

"Well, then she's got a nerve. Just you wait until she comes with that granddaughter of hers. I'll give her a piece of my mind. Pretending she could guarantee you a big celebrity, letting everybody make plans, just so she could feel important."

"There has to be more to it than that," Caiti insisted unhappily. "Nana is Griffon Falconer's grandmother. Besides, I've worked on the committee with her for months, and she's never seemed insecure or hungry for attention. If anything, she avoids the spotlight. It just doesn't make sense!"

"Well, sense or not, it leaves you in a pickle. The festival's set for next Saturday. The tickets are already sold. And what about all the donations people have sent?"

"We'll send them back," Caiti said firmly. "I appreciate the time you've put in, helping us keep track of the money, but we'll just have to send it all back."

"That's easy to say, but how? Those envelopes haven't all had return addresses on them, and a lot of people sent cash. And who's going to pay for all that return postage? The Neighborhood? You? If you ask me, that Mrs. Billinger ought to be the one. After all, she's the cause of the trouble."

"Let's just wait until she gets here," Caiti pleaded. "Maybe there's another way."

With a skeptical sniff, Mrs. Ames settled herself behind the counter and opened the ledger book to start her morning's work. "But why won't he?" she asked suddenly.

Caiti turned to her, surprised. "What?"

"Even if he didn't know what he was supposed to do for the fund-raiser before, don't you suppose that nice Mr. Falconer could be talked into cooperating? It would certainly be good publicity for his show."

It all sounded depressingly familiar. Caiti sighed. "I wouldn't set my heart on it if I were you, Mrs. Ames. They say nothing's certain but death and taxes, but the smart money says Griffon Falconer will leave town with his beard intact."

Mrs. Ames bent over her ledger again. "Well, after all the work you've done, I just think it's a crying shame."

Caiti sat down, pressing her icy fingers to the incipient ache at her temples. "It's nice to know there's somebody on my side. And it's even nicer not to have to spend my Saturdays struggling with debits and credits. Hiring you is one of the smartest things Papa Tony ever did. I don't know how we stayed in business without you to keep the books straight."

"Don't be silly. You did just fine."

"We got by," Caiti amended.

Mrs. Ames shrugged. "I know a survivor when I see one, and Antonio Buonarroti is a survivor. Having me in once a week to do the books and keep an eye on the front door may make your lives a little easier, but it isn't anything earthshaking."

"I wouldn't be too sure about that, Mrs. Ames. Lately, when Papa Tony looks at you, I've seen a sparkle in his eyes that I thought was gone forever."

"Don't tease an old woman, Caitlin. That man will still be flirting with the ladies when they nail his coffin shut. He never met a stranger."

"True. But that doesn't mean he has many friends. Not real ones. Papa Tony's lost a lot in his life. It isn't easy for him to let his guard down and get really close to anyone again. Safer just to be a 'pal' and have everybody say what a happy guy Tony Buonarroti is."

"Reminds me of somebody else in this room," Mrs. Ames said pointedly.

Caiti closed her eyes as tears threatened. "I don't know where I would have gone, what I would have done after Angelo died, if Papa Tony hadn't let me move in here with him...."

The bells over the door jingled, announcing a customer. Caiti sank lower in her chair, leaving Mrs. Ames to deal with the newcomer.

"Well, hello there!" Mrs. Ames exclaimed in tones of delight. "Are you here to have your picture taken?"

"Yes, ma'am." The answering voice was so breathless and high that Caiti stood up in surprise to see who had come in.

A little girl stood just inside the door, clutching a large stuffed bear. Freckles spilled across her tiny nose, and pale lashes fringed her wide hazel eyes. Her braids were auburn, fastened in green velveteen bows that matched her dress. White tights and shiny black Mary Janes completed the picture.

Mrs. Ames beamed at her. "What's your name, sweetheart?"

The little girl consulted the tops of her shoes and recited, in a careful singsong, "Mar-i-on Mar-ga-ret Fal-con-er...but you can call me Peggy. Nana says Peggy comes from the Margaret part."

So this was Nana Billinger's granddaughter...or, more likely, her great-granddaughter, Caiti reflected in surprise. Had she misunderstood when Nana made the appointment?

"And what's your friend's name, Peggy?" Mrs. Ames asked.

"Arthur," she said, hugging the bear in question.

Caiti looked expectantly at the door, but no adult entered. "Where's Nana, Peggy?"

"Home."

Exchanging glances of confusion with Mrs. Ames, Caiti tried again. "Who brought you, then?"

"Griffon. He said he'd be right back."

Griffon Falconer, here? The thought of facing him again was a daunting one, but it seemed there was no escape.

"How old are you, Peggy?"

"Four."

"And how old is Arthur?"

"Three," Peggy confided. "How old are you?"

Caiti smiled ruefully, hearing Mrs. Ames chuckle from behind the counter. "I'm twenty-seven. That's this many—" she held up all her fingers "—and this many again, and then seven. My name's Caiti. I'm going to take your picture today. Would Arthur like to have his picture taken, too?"

"Yes, please."

"Well, as soon as Griffon gets here, we'll go take his picture and your picture and Arthur's picture."

"He won't let you."

"Why not? Come on, Arthur. Please?"

"Not Arthur," Peggy corrected loftily. "Griffon. He told Nana pictures were silly."

"Oh, he did, did he? Well, we'll see about that when he gets here. While we wait for him, would you like to sit up on the counter so you can see out the window?"

"Could I?" Peggy's eyes grew round. "Arthur, too?"

"I think so. Let me check." Standing up, Caiti examined the surface of the counter. "Yes indeed. The sign here says that it's reserved for Princess Peggy and her escort, Crown Prince Arthur."

Peggy dissolved into giggles.

Caiti lifted the little girl up to sit on the counter, trying to reconcile herself to the unlikely knowledge that the tiny preschooler must be either Griffon's sister or his daughter. She certainly had Griff's hair. But not his eyes. These wide hazel eyes were nothing like Griff's dark chocolate gaze. Were they, instead, her mother's eyes? Denise's eyes?

Was that what Griff had been about to say, in the foyer? *"Caiti, this is Denise, my. . ."* What? Wife? Or, remembering the antipathy between them, perhaps his ex-wife?

"Your face is red," Peggy observed, then caroled, "Here he comes!"

The bells over the door jingled again. Swinging Peggy to the floor, Caiti braced herself as the rich tones of The Voice exclaimed, "Peg-o'-my-heart! And, unless I miss my guess, the lovely and elusive Ms Caitlin Kelly."

3

TURNING, Caiti saw that, except for the bright blaze of his hair and beard, Griff was a study in monochrome: black turtleneck sweater, black denim pants and a gray corduroy jacket. Even his deep brown eyes appeared black as he smiled at Caiti. *He's nothing to you,* she told herself. *A stranger.* Heedless, the adrenaline sang in her veins.

Then another bright head entered her line of sight: Peggy. And, by implication, Denise.

The tremors of excitement in Caiti's blood faded to a wary stillness.

Slowly Griff's mobile features shifted from an expression of delight to one of mischief. "'Rejoice with me,'" he declaimed, "'for I have found my sheep which was lost.'"

"I wasn't lost," Caiti said firmly, "I'm not a sheep, and I'm not yours."

His impish expression softened. "Sorry. No offense intended. Personally I'm rather fond of sheep. In fact, some of my best friends—"

"Do you always leave four-year-olds to wander around San Francisco by themselves?" Caiti demanded to silence his nonsense.

"Only when they're wearing their best dress and I'm hunting a parking space in the rain without an umbrella," he answered patiently.

Peggy tugged at Griff's hand. "Pick me up! Pick me up! I want to ride on your shoulders!"

He obliged her absently, intent on Caiti. "All in all, you don't look very pleased to see me." He cocked his head, wincing slightly as Peggy took a one-handed grip on his fiery curls. "Not that I'm surprised. Yesterday—" Flicking a glance at Mrs. Ames, he dropped his voice to a murmur. "Yesterday, after you left, I did a lot of thinking about what you told me," he said softly, as if a loud noise might cause Caiti to disappear again. "Can we try to work something out?"

"No hard feelings, but I think it would be better if I dealt with your grandmother. Really."

He came a step closer. "I'm sorry if I yelled at you yesterday. Don't you think we should talk?"

"I don't know," she said helplessly. Part of her wanted nothing more than to sit down with him and search for a solution to their dilemma. But the rest of her wanted to flee upstairs, leaving Mrs. Ames to sort out the whole unhappy tangle of motives and emotion. Torn, she stood her ground, watching Griff's slow approach.

"You aren't listed in the phone book," he said.

"I know." Why wouldn't her heart stop pounding and let her think?

"I asked Nana how I could find you, but she wouldn't tell me. She just kept insisting that I bring Peggy here today so some idiot could take her picture. I was ready to wring her neck!" An incredulous smile illuminated his face, spurring Caiti's pulse again. "But here I am. And, somehow, here you are, too." He gestured uncertainly at the reception area and the sign above the counter: Buonarroti Studios: By Appointment Only. "But how? What are you doing here, Caitlin?"

"Isn't it obvious?" Caiti asked, wishing her shifting emotions would reach a consensus. "I'm the 'idiot' who takes the pictures."

Griff closed his eyes in embarrassment. "Damn."

"Nana says that's a bad word," Peggy announced, tugging at his hair.

"Right you are. What I meant to say was 'Oops.'"

"Oops!" Peggy parroted. "Oops!"

Opening his eyes, Griff grimaced apologetically at Caiti. "Open mouth, insert foot, chew gently and swallow."

Behind the counter, Mrs. Ames could contain her curiosity no longer. "Aren't you Griffon Falconer?"

"Right you are," Griff said, smiling at her. "And you're . . . ?"

"Henrietta Ames. I'm a big fan of yours, Mr. Falconer." She turned to Caiti. "He's tall, but you didn't say he was so thin! I imagined he'd be a big burly lumberjack of a man! No offense, Mr. Falconer."

"None taken. We can't all be linebackers."

"And you can quit worrying—if Caiti hasn't hit you yet, she probably won't."

"You're sure about that?"

"It's considered poor form to bruise the customers," Caiti said, the uncertainty in her mind wavering toward hope. He certainly didn't act like a man with a guilty conscience.

Griff was grinning. "I dare to breathe again. So. Can we get together privately and talk, once you've taken Peggy's picture?"

"That depends," Caiti said, her thoughts racing.

"On what?"

There didn't seem to be any subtle way to find out. "Griff, is Peggy. . . ?"

When she didn't finish her questions, he prompted her, his face alive with curiosity. "Is she what? What do you need to know, Caiti?" A slow smile warmed his face. "Just ask. Don't be afraid. Not of me."

Her apprehension faded in the glow of his open expression. "Griff . . . what relation is Peggy to you?"

"Piglet here? She's my baby sister," he said, looking nonplussed. "Why?"

Caiti steeled herself. "And Denise?"

"She's Peggy's mother," he answered, bewildered but cooperative. "And my stepmother, since you ask. Why the sudden burning interest in our family tree?"

Before Caiti could answer, Peggy leaned down precariously to whisper in Griff's ear. Coloring, he lifted her down and confided, "The junior member says she needs to use the bathroom. Do you suppose that could be arranged?"

"I'll take her," Mrs. Ames offered. "This way, sweetheart."

Peggy looked up at Griff.

"Go ahead, Peggity Pete. I'll be right here when you come back," he promised.

"Can Arthur come?"

"Arthur wouldn't miss it for the world," Griff assured her gravely. "Run along now, before you spring a leak."

Reassured, Peggy took Mrs. Ames's hand and followed her docilely out of the room.

"Alone at last!" Griff exulted as the door closed behind them. "Quick, now, before they come back—any more questions?"

Find out, once and for all, the demon voice inside her insisted. *You'll never have the nerve again.* Caiti took a deep breath. "Are you married?" she asked and waited for the sky to fall.

Griff's laughter was as rich as his speaking voice. "In a word, no. I've tried a lot of things in my life, but marriage isn't one of them. Did you honestly think I might be? No, cancel that question. The look on your face when I walked in here is all the answer I need." His voice dropped to a conspiratorial whisper. "Had you decided who the unlucky lady might be?"

Chagrined, Caiti nodded. "Denise."

Griff whistled in deprecation. "That *would* have made me a cad!"

"A veritable bounder," Caiti agreed, smiling at the old-fashioned word.

"Dear heaven, woman, you cut me to the quick! Denise, no less! Bad enough to think I had the morals of an alley cat without accusing me of rotten taste, as well. For the record, I'm not married, engaged or romantically entangled—nor, for that matter, have I ever been, at least not seriously."

Caiti's spirits lifted.

"Your Honor," Griff said softly, "it is my contention that we've established beyond a reasonable doubt that the defendant is innocent of the charges brought against him. Defense counsel therefore respectfully requests that this case be dismissed and further requests the pleasure of your company at dinner tonight. After all, we have a fundraiser to discuss."

Dinner tonight.

Caiti opened her mouth to accept, then hesitated. She wanted to say yes, to spend the evening with him, to bask in the warmth of his attention and listen to the honeyed flattery of The Voice. But was she really ready to test her newfound equilibrium? With care and caution, she had built a life for herself, a life bounded by her work for Papa Tony and her involvement with The Neighborhood. Introducing Griff into that tranquil pattern, however tentatively, would be madness. The attraction she felt for him was already out of control, if last night's fevered dreams were any indication.

"Please?" he coaxed, coming closer.

Yes, no, yes, no . . . She squared her shoulders. "Thank you, Griff, but I can't."

"Tomorrow night, then?" he asked, undaunted.

"No. Thank you."

"Why not?" He eyed her apprehensively. "Is there someone *I* should know about?"

"No. I just can't."

"Why not?" he asked again.

"I don't date."

"Why not?"

She shook her head. "I just . . . don't. And don't keep saying 'Why not.'"

He grinned. "Why not?"

Feeling her resolve weakening, she quoted his own words back at him. "If we knew each other better, I'd ask you to take me on faith. But to do that now would be presump—"

"All right," he interrupted with a groan. "Point taken. If I've got a right to make decisions without explaining them, so do you." He caught both her hands in his. "But something happens to me when I'm around you, Caiti. Don't you feel it? Can't you see what it's doing to me? Whatever it is, I don't want it to stop. I just want—"

"No!" Caiti protested in alarm. If she listened, if she let him go on, she'd start believing his lovely fantasies. The Voice had that power; whatever words it spoke sounded believable, even inevitable. But in an hour the show ended, and reality began again. Reality was Papa Tony's studio and her work with The Neighborhood. Reality was the memory of Angelo.

"Why does that frighten you?" Griff stroked his thumbs slowly over the backs of her hands. "If anybody's scared, it should be me! But I'm the man they pay to spin romances over the airwaves to millions of faceless listeners every week. How can I fold my tent and walk meekly away, just when all those words are starting to make sense? You intrigue me, Caiti. When I look at you—"

"No, Griff."

"Yes! Caiti, I want to explore what we could have together. Is that such a terrible thing? Don't you want it, too? Aren't you curious about who we could be, if we gave ourselves the chance?"

"There's nothing to be curious about."

"Then why did you care whether I was married?"

Before she could frame a coherent reply, Peggy burst back into the room, with Mrs. Ames in tow. "They've got little white soaps just like Nana's roses!" Peggy told Griff, holding up her hands. "Smell!"

Kneeling, Griff made an elaborate show of sniffing Peggy's hands, front and back, snuffling like a bloodhound while Peggy giggled and Mrs. Ames beamed indulgently. "Just like Nana's roses," he agreed.

The two auburn heads made a lovely picture together, as did their obvious delight in each other. Caiti watched them, grateful for the distraction. Lovely pictures, after all, were the reason for their presence at Buonarroti Studios. It was a question of business, not pleasure. But Griff wasn't an easy man to refuse. She would feel safer with a camera between herself and Griff's dark eyes. "Are you ready now?" she asked them.

Peggy nodded enthusiastically, braids flying.

"Then come on. Let's get started."

Standing up, Griff turned Peggy around and gave her a little push toward Caiti. "Go ahead, pumpkin. I'll be back for you in a little while."

"You're welcome to stay and watch," Caiti said. "For that matter, I could take some shots of the two of you together, if you like."

"No. Thanks, anyway."

But the prospect of having Griff as a subject was too heady to give up on without a struggle. Through the camera, she always viewed the world with fresh eyes. And she was in sore need of objectivity where Griff was concerned. "It's painless," she promised, smiling. "Won't you reconsider?"

Griff's answering smile was distant. "No, thanks. A picture of Peggy is all we need."

Peggy's lower lip was trembling again. "But it's for Nana's *birth*day."

"Nana knows what I look like," Griff said with weary patience. "She doesn't need a picture of me."

Peggy's tiny chin lifted stubbornly. "Then I don't want anybody to take *my* picture, either."

Griff pointed a stern finger at Peggy's bear. "Arthur, I thought you and I had a gentleman's agreement. You were supposed to explain to Peggy that she's still growing up. She'll look different next year, and different again, the year after that. That's why Nana needs a picture of her, so she can always remember what Peggy looked like when she was four. But I'm a grown-up. I looked the same last year, and I'll look the same next year, and the next year, and the year after that. Nana doesn't need a picture of me."

"But she'd like one. I *know* she would!" Peggy wailed, and the tears brimmed visibly in her eyes.

Griff turned to Caiti. "Don't just stand there," he stage-whispered. "Help!"

"But she'd like it," Caiti echoed mischievously. "I *know* she would."

"Fat lot of help you are," he groaned, kneeling beside Peggy. When he spoke again, his voice was thick with the lilt of the Irish. "Blessed Michael and all the saints, Marion Margaret Falconer, is that a tear I see shining in your eye?"

Peggy nodded and sniffed.

"Oh, Pegeen, light of my life, heart of my heart, you wouldn't be after doing that to me, now, would you? Don't you know what would become of me if one of those tears should slip over and trickle down your cheek?"

"What?" Peggy asked, momentarily distracted.

"The very heart in my breast would melt in two at the sight of it," Griff insisted, "and where would we ever be finding glue enough to stick the two halves of it together again, one to the other, I ask you?"

"You're silly," Peggy pronounced, and Caiti saw the corners of her mouth begin to tilt upward.

"Yes," Griff agreed, the brogue abruptly absent from his tongue, "I'm silly. I'm also stubborn. And you've kept Caiti waiting long enough. Go with her, now, and take Arthur with you, and I'll be back in half an hour to take you out for ice cream." He stuck out his hand. "Deal?"

Peggy kept both her hands wrapped firmly around her bear. "Me and Arthur want you to stay."

"Arthur and I," Griff corrected. "And the answer is no."

"Please?"

He hesitated.

"Just to watch?" Peggy entreated. "So me and Arthur won't be scared here, all alone, and cry?"

"I've created a monster," Griff said, and threw his hands skyward in surrender. "All right, I'll stay." He shot a warning glance at Caiti. "But just to watch. Got that, Arthur? Just to watch."

"AND THAT'S EXACTLY what he did," Caiti told Papa Tony as they cleared the dinner table. "Stood behind me and watched." Cradling the salt and pepper shakers in her palm, she remembered the warmth of Griff's nearness, the electric sense of intimacy as he stepped up close behind her and gazed over her shoulder, cajoling his little sister into smiling naturally for the camera. "I got some wonderful shots of Peggy. I even brought her up here and posed her in the window seat, with the raindrops on the glass behind her." Caiti smiled at the memory of auburn hair and deep green velvet against the cool gray of the rain-streaked window. "But Nana's going to have to get along without a portrait of her grandson."

"He sounds like an angry young man," Papa Tony said thoughtfully. "Angry or unhappy."

Caiti turned to him, astonished. "Griff? Oh, no, Papa, he's not like that at all! Griffon Falconer's a very bright man. Very talented. He has a wonderful sense of humor."

Papa Tony shrugged. "From what you say, he spends his life saying no to things—helping with your fund-raiser, having his picture taken . . . To turn away from new experiences is not the action of a happy man." He raised his eyebrows. "Especially when the new experiences are offered to him by a beautiful young woman."

"I'm not beautiful," Caiti protested, coloring at the thought of Griff's insistent attentions.

"Then the photographs I have taken of you lie."

Setting the little glass shakers on the cupboard shelf, Caiti smiled lovingly at Papa Tony. "All your photographs are lies," she told him. "Beautiful, generous lies. That's why people come to have Antonio Buonarroti shoot their portraits. They know what a magician you are."

Papa Tony shook his head in protest. "The camera does not lie, it selects. There are a dozen, a hundred sides to each person. When I choose to photograph a side that is not easily visible to the world, that side is no less real than the others." He shook a handful of silverware at her, his gaze growing more intense. "Your beauty is no lie, Caitlin. It is there, however you try to smother it. You are a young girl, with the rest of your life before you. The camera sees that beauty, that promise in you."

Caiti turned away, afraid of the anguish in his eyes because she knew its cause. Her life with Papa Tony, their work together, side by side, was anchored in the loss they shared, a pain so profound that it was rarely mentioned. Only sometimes, when the need was great and one of them was feeling strong enough . . .

"Angelo saw it, too," Papa Tony said quietly. "He was the first to see it, and he saw it most clearly. Do you think he would want you to deny that beauty, that spirit, and grow no more? Perhaps it was unfair of me to keep you here—"

"Unfair?" Caiti's throat tightened. "Papa, you can't believe that. Where would I have gone? What would I have done without you?"

"How will you ever know, unless you search out those answers for yourself? Perhaps you should try your wings."

In the silent kitchen, the warmth of Caiti's sweater was suddenly stifling. "I'm sorry," she said, willing her voice to be steady. "Of course I'll move out, if that's what you think I should do. I never meant to be a burden to you."

"A burden?" The chair creaked as Papa Tony dropped his weight into it. "You are a joy to me, Caitlin. And your work in the studio is as good as my own! But I want what is best for you," he insisted. "Now and always."

"I know you do," Caiti said placatingly. "Please don't worry about me. I'm fine."

"You are alone."

"I have you."

"That isn't what I mean."

She shrugged in frustration. "Be fair. You make it sound as if I've locked myself away. I meet new people every day here at the studio."

"Families," Papa Tony said dismissively. "Or young girls who have come for their wedding portraits."

"I see the other volunteers from The Neighborhood."

"Old women like Marion Billinger."

"Not all of them. Besides, they're good people. Friends are important, Papa."

"So is love."

Sighing, Caiti went to him. "So is love," she agreed. "But it isn't always easy to find, as you know perfectly well." She bent to kiss his plump cheek. "Well, I'd better go. I've still got work to do. Thank you for dinner. It was delicious."

"You do not eat enough," he scolded.

"And you worry too much. I'll be in the darkroom if you want me. Sweet dreams, Papa."

"Good night, Caitlin. Will you forgive me for being a bossy old man?"

"The only thing I wouldn't forgive you for is not caring," she assured him, and let herself into the dark stairwell.

She wished Papa Tony would think more about himself and less about her. After the accident, it was true that there had been a time, a long, hard time, when memories of Angelo were more than she could face. But that was three years past. The sharp pain of loss had dulled gradually to a bittersweet ache that seemed a proper and in-

tegral part of her. The goal wasn't to forget. The goal was
to remember and yet find the strength and will to face the
future.

It wasn't easy; it wasn't supposed to be. When Angelo
died, Papa Tony lost his son, his only child. And she—she
had been deprived of lover, husband and friend, the man
who completed her days, the boy she had loved since she
was nine years old. But she and Papa Tony still had each
other and their work. And life went on, as rich and varied
as it had always been, full of pain and joy and possibility.

The Neighborhood had helped her immeasurably in her
attempt to learn how to live without Angelo. Within days
of his death, one of their members had visited her hospital room, not with a lecture but with a disarming willingness to listen to her as she talked through her sense of
trauma and loss. As the days turned to weeks, and then to
months, their support of her had been as unflagging as
their patience, and the opportunities they offered her to
take part in Neighborhood projects sharpened her realization that she was not alone in her misfortune.

Over time, the chance to do something constructive for
others had proved to be the best grief therapy of all. It was
a way of fighting back against the blind malevolence of
chance, however indirectly. Privately, within her heart,
she dedicated every act of kindness, every hour of aid to
Angelo's memory, and took comfort in the legacy of care
she was creating.

As to the rest, she could honestly say she was doing her
best to embrace the possibilities life sent her way…couldn't
she?

The sudden shrill buzzing of the doorbell made her
jump.

At seven o'clock on a Saturday night? Caiti asked herself in surprise. The studio was locked and dark, with the

Closed sign hanging in plain view. Why would anyone be trying to get in?

The buzzer sounded again.

Reaching the bottom step, she unlocked the inner door of the studio, moving surely in the darkness. The shop and the apartment behind it were her home, now, and Papa Tony was all the family she needed. How could leaving all that behind possibly be "best" for her?

The doorbell was buzzing out a pattern: three short bursts, three long blasts that made her molars ache, then three short bursts again. An SOS.

Bewildered and concerned, Caiti hurried to the door. Was someone hurt? In trouble? Drawing back a corner of the curtain, she looked out and gaped in astonishment at what she saw.

Griffon Falconer stood waiting on the doorstep.

As the curtain moved in her hand, Griff abandoned his assault on the doorbell and pressed his nose to the glass. "Caiti?" he mouthed. "Help!"

Switching off the alarm, Caiti unlocked the door and opened it for him, her heart racing. "Griff! What are you doing here?"

"Major-league disaster," Griff groaned, slipping inside.

Caiti's stomach lurched. "Is your grandmother all right?"

"Nana, for once, is the least of my problems."

"Then what is it?" Caiti demanded, closing the door, her fingers moving over the locks automatically. "What's wrong?"

"Arthur's missing!"

"Arthur?" She stared at him blankly for a moment. Then, as her anxiety turned to indignation, she snapped, "You scared me half to death over a misplaced bear?"

Griff matched her outraged expression and bettered it. "You've obviously never dealt with the four-year-old mind—or, at least, with Peggy's four-year-old mind. Chaos does not begin to describe what's been going on since we discovered that Arthur'd gone over the wall. I've spent the past hour and a half retracing our steps. Did you ever try to get into the zoo after hours? Or F.A.O. Schwartz? Thank God I didn't take her to Alcatraz today, or she'd expect me to swim over and check out the cell block!" He glared at her with mock ferocity. "Think it's funny, do you?"

Caiti put her hand over her traitorous mouth. "I'm sorry, Griff, I'm not laughing at you, really I'm not—"

Griff's mustache tilted as he grinned. "As Nana would say, 'It's no laughing matter, but it's no matter if you laugh.' I'll admit, I've spent evenings doing saner things than searching San Francisco for a missing bear." His grin softened to a tender smile. "But Arthur really is gone, and Peggy really is upset. And I really have spent the past hour and a half pounding the pavement, to no avail." He moved closer, a shadowy height in the dimness. "You're my last hope," he said softly.

Caiti looked up at him. The glow of streetlights through the window picked out the sweeping curve of his cheekbone, austere above the fullness of his beard. "Am I, Griff?"

"Absolutely." For a moment, he leaned closer still, and Caiti took an unsteady breath, hungry for the touch of him. But he turned away, and the tension between them evaporated. "So how about it, lady? Think there might be a bear on the premises?"

"We can look," she promised, relieved and disappointed. "I haven't tripped over him anywhere, but—"

The light on the landing snapped on, painfully bright, and Papa Tony's voice boomed down the narrow stairwell. "Caitlin? Are you all right? Who was at the door?"

"I'm fine, Papa." Pulling Griffon with her, Caiti went to the foot of the stairs, stepping into the circle of light. "This is Griffon Falconer, Nana Billinger's grandson. Griff, I'd like you to meet Antonio Buonarroti."

Griff nodded politely. "Pleased to meet you, sir."

"And what is it that we can do for you, Mr. Falconer?"

"I'm looking for a bear, sir."

"Looking for *what*?"

Caiti smiled. "It's all right, Papa. Griff's little sister lost her stuffed bear and he thinks she may have left it here. We're going to look for it. It won't take long."

Papa Tony made a noncommittal sound and withdrew, leaving the stairway light on.

Griff smiled and shook his head. "I don't think he's convinced. Isn't he used to clients hunting for their bears?"

"Frankly, I think this is a first."

"Maybe that's why he left the light on—so you could keep an eye on me. Something about you seems to inspire people's protective instincts."

"What's that supposed to mean?" Caiti asked, switching on the lights in the reception area.

He stroked his beard protectively. "Just that I don't think I'm Nana's favorite grandchild at the moment." Shrugging out of his jacket, he looked around the room. "So. Where do we start?"

"Right here," Caiti said, and knelt to search under the counter. "You make it sound like Nana's going to sit on you while we pull your beard out a fistful at a time."

"Don't give her any ideas. She'd be willing."

"Why?" Caiti asked. "Does she prefer her men clean shaven?"

"Do you?"

Standing up, Caiti dusted her palms together. "No sign of Arthur here," she said, dodging his question. "Let's try the studio."

"'Lay on, Macduff.'" He followed her down the hallway. "By the way, Nana wants to meet with you tomorrow, if you've got the time."

"Good," Caiti said, flicking the switch that controlled the studio lights. "She and I need to talk."

Except for the free-standing lights and the camera and tripod in the middle of the floor, the studio was basically an empty room. The walls boasted a variety of backdrops: matte black, soft mottled blue, an impressionistic meadow scene. . . .

"I don't see any sign of Arthur," Griff said, sighing. "Strike three."

"Don't be a pessimist. Let's check behind the backdrops before we give up. You take that wall. I'll start here."

Crossing the room, Griff made a wide detour around the tripod, then cast a guilty look over his shoulder at Caiti. "You shouldn't leave a thing like that lying around," he quipped, jerking his thumb at the camera. "It might be loaded."

She shook her head in rueful despair. "How did FineArts ever talk you into having your picture taken?"

"They did what any reasonable employer would— threatened to give the show to someone else if I didn't cooperate."

Caiti laughed.

Griff folded his arms, the dark sleeves of his turtleneck blending with the backdrop. "I'm serious."

"But that's blackmail!"

"Tell me about it."

"Besides, 'Heroes & Heartbreakers' wouldn't be the same without you."

"Thanks for the vote of confidence, but all this was happening two years ago, when the show was just getting off the ground. By all accounts, I was eminently replaceable. From where I stood, it looked like a pretty clear choice between having my picture taken or going back to doing commercial voice-overs. So they took the picture." The lights threw his silhouette onto the blue backdrop. "But I've got more clout now. I don't have to put up with that kind of pressure. Not on the show, anyway."

If he hadn't been so visibly distressed, she would have laughed again. "Griff, it's just a photograph. No big deal."

"If it's no big deal, why does everybody keep—" He threw his hands up in disgust. "Forget it. Arthur isn't here. I may as well go home."

"I don't see what you're so upset about," Caiti persisted. "All right, FineArts chose an underhanded way of getting what they wanted from you. But you can't seriously compare that to Nana's motives in sending you here."

Griff turned away, stubbornly silent.

"Nana's a sweet old woman who'd like a portrait of her grandson. You're in New York most of the time, and she misses you. Is that so hard to understand?"

Griff turned back to face her. "Have a heart," he entreated. "Every time you analyze my motives, I end up sounding like a cross between Genghis Khan and Simon Legree." The laugh lines around his mouth deepened. "Present evidence to the contrary, I'm not an irretrievably rotten person. I'm even cooperative, on occasion. But Nana has a genius for getting what she wants out of me, and from time to time it brings out my stubborn streak."

"But you love her," Caiti supplied, "which makes it hard to say no to her."

"But I love her," he conceded, "which makes it damn near impossible to say no to her. Oh, well. What price pride? Far be it from me to blight my grandmother's fading years. I'll have the damn picture taken."

"Good. When?"

Griff shot her a hunted look. "Before I go back to New York," he stated. "Okay?"

"Fine. How about now?"

"Now?"

She shrugged. "You're here. I'm here. The camera's here. Why not just bite the bullet and get it over with?"

GRIFF'S GAZE slid from her face to the camera and back again. "That's quite an offer," he observed, his tone poised awkwardly between flirtation and anxiety. "Are you sure you want me as a subject?"

"I'm sure," Caiti said.

Griff lifted his hands in mock surrender. "So be it, then. What do I do?"

Lifting a wooden stool from its place against the wall, she set it in front of the blue backdrop. "Come over here, for starters. Have a seat. We can begin with a few head and shoulder shots."

"What kind of camera is that?" Griff said, perching gingerly on the stool as she adjusted the lights and swiveled the camera on its tripod.

"It's a Bronica." Caiti brought his image into focus. "Turn a little to your left."

"Hmm. I've heard of Kodak and Nikon and Canon, but I've never heard of . . . What was it again?"

"A Zenza Bronica SLR."

"SLR?"

"Single lens reflex." Working quickly, she repositioned the reflector umbrellas and stepped behind the camera again. "Try lowering your chin. . . . Yes." A stab of pleasure flashed through her as the composition she had envisioned fell into place. "Okay, hold it right there. . . ."

But Griff's head jerked up at the sound of footsteps overhead.

"It's only Papa Tony," Caiti explained.

"He lives up there?" Griff asked, examining the ceiling with exaggerated interest.

"Yes. His apartment's on the second floor and mine's down here, behind the studio."

"Convenient. Must make for a quick commute."

Caiti bit back an exasperated sigh. "Come on, Griff, look this way. You're harder to pose then Peggy!"

"Peggy claims there are ceiling creatures," he said lightly, still looking up. "She says they make funny faces at her, and that's why she laughs in church."

"A little cooperation . . . ?"

"Sorry. You're right."

Revealed through the lens, Griff's bone structure was classic in its purity: high, broad forehead, arched brows, dramatic cheekbones. . . .

"Relax," Caiti coaxed, and pressed the shutter release.

His nose was neither long nor short, neither broad nor thin. The nostrils were neatly sculpted, twin curves above his flourishing mustache. And his chin—Caiti sighed in frustration. Who could tell anything about his chin? It was hidden, buried beneath a wilderness of beard. In the midst of that auburn thicket, his mouth was an isolated oasis, the upper lip pressed unsmilingly to the lower in silent displeasure at her scrutiny.

The shutter clicked again.

Griff jerked slightly at the sound, the stiff set of his features growing even grimmer.

Straightening, Caiti stepped toward him, putting herself between Griff and the camera lens.

"Is that it?" he asked, brightening. "Are we done?"

"We haven't even started. Not really. Have a heart, Griff. What I've taken so far might do for a Wanted poster, but I don't think that's what Nana had in mind."

"No, of course not," he said, looking genuinely abashed.

"Let's try again, then."

"Any suggestions?"

"Well," she said, going back to her camera, "you could try a smile, for starters."

It was a change, but not an improvement. "You look as if somebody's standing just out of camera range, pointing a gun at your head," she lamented, after a few fruitless minutes.

"Sorry. I guess I'm just not photogenic."

"No, it isn't that. Not with those bones. But you're getting in your own way. You don't trust the camera, and it shows. What's the matter? Afraid I'm going to raffle off the negatives at the fund-raiser?"

"I wouldn't blame you if you did," he said bleakly. "Let's just forget the photographs, okay, Caiti? I'll give Nana something else for her birthday. I came here tonight to find Arthur, not to waste your time."

"It's my time," Caiti pointed out, walking slowly to the stool where he sat. "And I don't think it's being wasted. I'd like to take your picture, Griff. But you'll have to relax and trust me."

Seated on the stool, he had forfeited his height advantage. Caiti could read the apprehension in his eyes, and the indecision, and, beneath it all, something else, glowing like an ember, flaring stronger as she watched, as if her own gaze were a breeze coaxing it toward flame.

"Maybe what I need is an incentive," he suggested.

"What do you mean?"

"Something to look forward to. Something... pleasant. Would you consider a trade?"

"That depends. What would we be trading?"

Griff's smile was as intimate as a touch. "Kisses for photographs?"

She knew she ought to dismiss his suggestion with a laugh, but his words woke an answering fire deep within her. After years of numb indifference, Caiti felt an unexpected thrill of excitement at the thought of Griffon's lips pressed to hers. She wanted to explore the tangle of strength and insecurity she sensed in him. She wanted to feel his arms around her. She wanted to abandon herself to the promises in his eyes.

There was danger in wanting those things, and even more danger in admitting her desires too freely. But she couldn't deny that for the second time in her life she was feeling the magical attraction of a woman for one special man. If she turned away from Griffon Falconer now, would she ever have such an opportunity again? And it was only a kiss, after all. Only a kiss.

It was a risk she was willing to run...within limits. With a final remnant of caution, she forced a light note into her voice and said, "All right, if that's your price. But I'll expect your full cooperation." Walking to the tripod, she detached her camera. "And I'll set the terms—three acceptable photographs, payment in advance."

"Three pictures in exchange for a kiss," he agreed. "Just remember, I'll be expecting your full cooperation, too."

Dry-mouthed, Caiti nodded.

"Fair enough," he said. "Let's get started."

"All right. Turn around."

"With my back to the camera?" he asked incredulously.

"For now, yes." Freed from the restrictions of the tripod, she stalked him slowly, searching for the best angles. "Keep your body still and turn your head toward me...." Her breath snagged as his face filled her vision. The stiff self-consciousness that had marred her first shots of Griff was gone, replaced by a look of vibrant longing. Focusing quickly, she captured it on the sensitive emulsion.

"That's one," said The Voice, heavy with anticipation.

Stepping closer, Caiti sank to one knee and refocused, holding her breath as she stroked the shutter release.

"Two," he counted, his lips lingering over the soft syllable.

Caiti could feel her heart beating in her throat. She stood up slowly, moving to her left. "Follow me with your eyes. And tilt your head a little to the side.... Oh, yes," she sighed, delighted. The shutter clicked.

"That makes three," Griff said, and the air between them seemed to shimmer as he smiled. "What's the verdict? Did you have my full cooperation?"

Caiti nodded, unwilling to trust her voice.

"Then I do believe it's my turn." Griff uncoiled from his perch on the stool. "Just relax," he coaxed, his tone a silky parody of her own.

Her hands were cold, her face burning.

"Follow me with your eyes," Griff instructed, but the order wasn't necessary. It was beyond her to look anywhere else. He was in front of her now, lifting the camera out of her hands, stooping to set it on the floor, then rising again, unfolding slowly to his full height. "And tilt your head a little to the side...." His beard tickled her chin as he bent his head. "Oh, yes," he said softly, and lowered his lips to hers.

As she closed her eyes and abandoned herself to the sweet urgency of Griff's kiss, Caiti's awareness of the room faded. For ten years, she had spent a part of nearly every day in the studio, surrounded by the familiar backdrops, the patched ceiling, the lights on their spindly, splay-footed poles. Blindfolded, she would still have recognized the unique scent of it. But all of that was falling away beneath

Griff's touch, leaving her stranded in the black velvet void of her own response.

The places where Griff was touching her became the points of a new compass. True north was the yearning of his mouth on hers, and the tantalizing feather-touch of his tongue as it explored her parting lips. East was the length of his left hand, from the smooth palm so warm against the exposed column of her throat to the delicate fingertip tracing the curves and hollows of her ear, sending shivers of desire through her. South was the glancing pressure of his lower body as she swayed against him, reawakening a long-dormant excitement that pulsed in her veins like May wine. And west . . . west was the tensile strength of Griff's right hand steadying her, his fingers encircling her side, his palm resting just below the curve of her breast, so near, so near. . . .

Footsteps overhead.

A whimper of protest rose in Caiti's throat as Griff lifted his mouth from hers and dropped his hands to his sides. "It's only Papa Tony—" she began, then stopped in surprise as the door at the head of the stairway creaked and the footsteps started their descent.

"Here." Red-faced, Griff bent to retrieve the camera and thrust it into her hands, "I'm sorry."

"Sorry? Sorry for what?"

But there was no more time. The doorway curtain swung aside and Papa Tony came into the studio, with Arthur under his arm.

"Is this the bear that was lost?" he asked cheerfully, then hesitated. His gaze flicked from Caiti to Griff, his pleased expression faltering. "Perhaps I am interrupting—"

Griff held out his hand. "That's the bear, all right. Where did you find him?"

Papa Tony beamed. "It was behind the draperies on the window seat. At dinner, Caitlin spoke of having posed the little girl there. When she did not come up to say that the two of you had found the bear, it occurred to me to look there for it."

"That's wonderful, sir," Griff said, and came forward to shake Papa Tony's hand and take custody of Arthur. "Thank you. Peggy will be glad to have him home safe and sound. It's already past her bedtime. Thank you for your help, sir." He turned to include Caiti in his thanks, his eyes belying the casual impersonality of his voice. "Thank you both. I'm sorry to have bothered you after the shop was closed."

Papa Tony led the way out into the reception area. "It was no bother." The locks clicked under his hands. "We were glad to be of help." He opened the door. "Well, a good night to you, Mr. Falconer. Drive carefully."

"Good night, Mr. Buonarroti," Griff said, lifting his jacket from the counter. "Good night, Caiti." But his gaze locked with hers, revealing his rueful dismay at Papa Tony's inexorable good manners. What could Griff do but leave, bear in hand?

"I'll walk you to your car," she offered, and was rewarded by the warmth of Griff's smile.

Papa Tony stared at her in surprise.

Taking her coat down from its hook, she shrugged into it and stepped past him onto the sidewalk, grateful for the cooling touch of the night air on her face. "You can go ahead and lock up, Papa. I've got my keys."

"I'll see that she gets back safely," Griff promised.

"Very well, then," Papa Tony said, and closed the door, leaving her alone again with Griff.

The rain had stopped, but the scent of it still hung in the air. The wet pavement gleamed in patches like dull black mirrors, mimicking the street lamps.

Griff slipped his arm through hers. "Thank you," he said, as they started down the sidewalk. "And, I'm sorry."

"For what?"

He kicked at a soggy piece of newspaper. "For putting you on the spot with Mr. Buonarroti like that, in the studio. I had no business kissing you. Not then. Not there."

Caiti laughed, relieved. "Don't worry. Papa Tony's my friend, not my keeper. He doesn't try to run my life."

Griff smiled at her with the air of a man willing to be convinced.

"I'm well past the age of consent," she reminded him, with a smile. "I decide for myself who I'll kiss, and when, and where. What happened between you and me in the studio is our business, not his. And he'd be the first to agree with that."

"But it's his studio," Griff reminded her. "You work for him. I just don't want you getting into trouble at your job because of me."

Caiti squeezed his arm. "Thank you. That's nice. But it really isn't something you need to worry about. He and I have an understanding."

"You're sure?"

"Absolutely. If there was any doubt about it, I'd say so. I think the world of Papa Tony. I don't know what I'd do without him."

"In that case," Griff said softly, "I think I envy him."

Not knowing how to respond, Caiti walked on in silence, refusing to focus on anything beyond the quiet of the night and the pleasure of Griff's arm under her hand. For once, the present moment was enough.

They reached the corner and turned it, walking past the silent doorways of the apartment buildings.

"Are you free tomorrow?" Griff asked.

Tomorrow. Sunday. The shop would be closed and her time would be her own. What better way to spend it than by sharing it with Griff? "Is that an invitation?"

"In a way." He pressed her hand closer against his side. "Being my devious grandmother's devious grandson, I'm plotting out how to have my cake and eat it, too."

"Meaning . . . ?"

"Nana's anxious to get together with you . . . but so am I. What would you say to meeting her for Sunday brunch and then letting me kidnap you for the afternoon?"

Caiti smiled. "I'd say it's the best offer I've had all week. What time should I be ready?"

Griff thought about it. "Would ten-thirty be too early?"

"Ten-thirty would be just fine. What should I wear?"

"Good question. It all depends. What's your pleasure? A drive along the coast? Window-shopping on Union Square?"

"Actually . . ."

"What? It's up to you. Really."

"Well, the Winship retrospective is in its last week at the Museum of Modern Art. I've been meaning to see it, if you'd be interested."

"Perfect," Griff applauded. "I missed it when it was in New York. That's settled, then. Dress for a leisurely stroll through the museum." He slowed, stopping at a double driveway. "I'm parked over there," he said, gesturing across the street, and Caiti recognized Nana's red Volvo in the glow of a street light. "Can I drive you back to the shop or would you rather just—"

Brakes squealing, a car rounded the corner on two wheels and sped toward them, kicking up spray from the damp street.

"*No!*" Caiti screamed in horror, and flung herself back into the shelter of a doorway, dragging Griff along with desperate strength.

Headlights flashed past.

She held her breath, straining to hear over the pounding of her heart.

The whine of the motor faded . . .

"Caiti?"

. . . faded . . .

"Caiti, are you all *right?*"

. . . faded to silence.

Her pulse began to slow. Reluctantly she opened her eyes.

His arms were wrapped around her, holding her close against the solid warmth of his chest. His fingers, buried in her hair, stroked the sensitive skin at the nape of her neck while he murmured a soft litany of reassurance. "It's okay, just some hot-rodding kid. He's gone now. You're safe. Don't be afraid. Everything's all right. . . ."

She was shaking—from reaction, from embarrassment, from the potent stimulus of his embrace. She didn't want to explain, didn't want to remember. All she wanted was to regain the fragile sense of happiness she had enjoyed a few short moments ago and wrap it close around her like a cloak to shut out the darkness and terror. Twisting in his grasp, she raised her face to his and drew him down with shaking hands. "Hold me," she whispered unsteadily against his lips. "Kiss me. Please."

He sheltered her with his body, kissing her with a fervor that left no room for fears, courting her lips with his.

She clung to him, overwhelmed as much by the tide of her own response as by the play of his mouth on hers.

When the fierce intensity of his arms around her eased, it was only to free his right hand for a journey from the nape of her neck to the flushed plane of her cheek and from there slowly down to cup the aching weight of her breast.

At his touch, Caiti closed her eyes more tightly, willing herself deeper into the enchantment. *Safe*, the voice within her exulted, as her hands stroked his back and her mouth gleaned a harvest of delight. *My love, my love, this time we kept each other safe....*

This time?

She woke to reality with a shiver.

It was Griffon's lips that kissed her, his clever fingers that caressed her body. However sweet that touch might be, it wasn't Angelo's and never could be. The past was not so easily cheated.

She held Griff tightly for an instant more, then drew back, still trapped within the circle of his arms.

"Caiti?" He tried to coax her close again. "Are you all right?"

She swallowed against the tightness in her throat. "I'm fine."

"Like hell you're fine. I can feel you shaking."

"It's nothing. Please. Papa Tony's waiting. I should go back—"

"No. Not while you're this upset. Come on. We'll sit in the car."

She shivered again and felt Griff's troubled scrutiny intensify. Without another word, he turned her toward the street, draping one arm protectively around her shoulders.

She took a few faltering steps at his insistence but balked at the curb.

"No cars coming," Griff said firmly, and guided her over the wet pavement with steady, measured steps.

By the time they reached the far curb, her legs would barely support her.

"Okay, hang on. Here we are, all in one piece." Griff braced her against the side of the car and unlocked the passenger door. "Come on, camera lady, sit down before you fall down."

She sank gratefully onto the vinyl upholstery.

"Here," Griff said, "hold on to Arthur. He's feeling a little shaky, too."

She sat there limply while he fastened the seat belt around her, his long-fingered touch oddly remote after the passion they had shared. When he was done, he closed her door and walked around the car, as shadowed as her memories.

Caiti watched him, feeling hollow and shivery, chilled by the sharp reminder of how fleeting life could be. A careless moment, a senseless accident, could end it forever.

She wasn't ready for her life to be over.

The dome light flared on and off as he opened his door and settled into the driver's seat. "Want to tell me about it?" he asked, and she felt his warm hands enfold her chilled ones.

Caiti drew a ragged breath.

"Sometimes it helps," he said mildly.

She searched for words that would tell him enough without endangering her precarious control. "A couple of years ago . . . I was . . . hit."

"By a car, you mean? A drunk driver?"

"Maybe. I don't know. It was hit-and-run. They never caught him." Her fingers cramped in Arthur's fur. "It was dark and rainy, like tonight. He just came out of no-

where. And then—" She took a deep breath, forcing a
smile when she saw Griff's concern. "I'm all right," she insisted. "It was just . . . too familiar." The last of the adrenaline faded from her blood, leaving an inexorable tide of
exhaustion in its place. "I'm all right," she repeated. "Just
tired."

Griff bent his head, and she felt his lips press gently to
her cold fingers. "I'm glad you had nine lives, sweet Cait.
Just rest. I'll take you home."

His hands left hers. Caiti heard the jingle of keys; then
the headlights glowed and the little engine came to life beneath Griff's touch.

He circled the block slowly, saying nothing, and Caiti
realized he was giving her time to pull herself back together. "Worst place in the whole city to try and find a
parking place," he muttered at last as he stopped the car,
double parked, in front of the studio. "You're sure you're
okay? I could walk you upstairs—"

"No, I'll be all right. I promise." Setting Arthur aside,
Caiti leaned across the seat and kissed Griff lightly. "I'll be
ready tomorrow at ten-thirty."

"Ten-thirty," he affirmed. "Go on, now. I'll wait here
until you're safe inside."

She moved briskly—up to the door, key in the lock, step
inside, lights on, door closed. Then, pulling back the curtain, she looked out at him again.

"Caitlin?" came Papa Tony's voice from upstairs. "You
are back?"

"Yes, Papa."

Outside, Griff raised his hand in farewell.

"I have made tea," Papa Tony announced. "Come upstairs and have a cup with me."

Last chance to change her mind. She could still open the door and ask Griff to come back; she could still welcome him into her apartment, into her heart, into her life....

"Caitlin?"

"Yes, Papa, I'll be right up," she called, and waved wistfully, watching as Griff drove away.

When he was gone from sight, she leaned wearily against the door, feeling dizzy and disoriented, as if someone had blindfolded her and pushed her down a flight of stairs. And yet, when she closed her eyes, it wasn't the memory of threatening headlights that rose to haunt her, but the longing in Griff's eyes and the gentle hunger of his touch against her skin.

Tomorrow. She would see him again tomorrow. And who knew what might happen then?

In the years since Angelo's death, she had lived a life as chaste as any nun, not from a sense of guilt or obligation to the dead but because she had found no man to rival the memories of joy that were Angelo's legacy. Instead she'd focused her energies on breathing life into The Neighborhood, and had taken comfort from her work with Papa Tony and, more recently, from her budding friendship with Nana. The new way of life she'd built for herself was a good one, safe and steady and productive.

But now, against all likelihood and expectation, Griffon Falconer had exploded onto her horizon, forcing everything into a bold new perspective.

Lost in thought, Caiti turned to climb the stairs and face Papa Tony's well-intentioned curiosity.

5

WHAT ARE YOU going to do about Griff Falconer?

When Caiti opened her eyes to rainy gray daylight on Sunday morning, the question was there, as if it had crouched all night beside her pillow, waiting for her to wake.

"I'm going to talk him into saving the fund-raiser," she said aloud and stumbled down the hallway to the bathroom for the shower that was her traditional morning jump-start.

But this morning the path of the lathered washcloth on her skin conjured a disconcerting memory of Griff's hand cupping her breast, and her attempts to plan her coming confrontation with Nana kept getting lost in a strange new self-awareness of the curves and angles of her own flesh.

A thought rose, unbidden, in her mind: she was falling in love with Griff Falconer.

"Don't be ridiculous," she protested to the white tile walls. "I hardly know the man."

Nevertheless . . .

Caiti pressed the washcloth to her face. Falling in love? She couldn't be. Falling in love took years—a lifetime! She and Angelo had gone to kindergarten together. They'd played in the same backyard, blown out each others' birthday candles. Angelo had sent her her first valentine, her first corsage, given her her first kiss. When they had finally sought a more adult expression of their love, his body had seemed almost as familiar to her as her own, and the act itself had been a joining of two long-intended halves into a single satisfying whole.

Troubled, Caiti stepped deeper into the spray, rinsing the soap from her skin.

Griff was a virtual stranger. In a week, he'd go back to New York, and her life would return to normal. And maybe that was just as well.

Cutting the flow of water, Caiti stepped out onto the bath mat and toweled herself dry with rough, efficient strokes. Would it really be just as well, if Griff walked out of her life? Was that what she wanted, or was she afraid to upset the balance of her life and risk her heart again?

Slipping into her robe, she wandered back down the hall. Opening her bedroom closet, she faced the clothes there with blank uncertainty, wondering what to wear for a Sunday brunch with Nana and a tour of the museum with Griff.

Maybe the gray wool jumper.

Wonderful idea, her thoughts mocked. *You'll look about eight years old.*

"The black dress, then. Black's sophisticated."

No more black. You promised Papa Tony.

"Well, what, then?"

Her hand drifted along the row of hangers, stopping finally near the end of the rod to hover over a dress that hung apart from the others, draped protectively in clear plastic.

Her birthday dress. Her Angelo dress.

It was elegantly simple, fashioned of soft gray-green challis. "It's the color of the hills when the first rains break the drought and everything comes alive again," Angelo had said when he chose it as her twenty-first birthday present, and Papa Tony had photographed her in it, capturing the way the smoky shade stressed the green of her

eyes and brought out the deepest auburn highlights in her
hair.

In a dream, she pushed the shrouding plastic away.

Wear it.

"I can't."

Of course you can. Wear it. It's beautiful.

"I know it's beautiful, but—"

Wear it.

Caiti's fingers closed over the soft material.

For Griff.

Slowly she drew the zipper down.

DRIVING DOWN Union Street, Griff stole another glance at
Caiti where she sat beside him on the front seat of the
Volvo. All his midnight worries had apparently been un-
necessary; whatever dark memories last night's misad-
venture had awakened in her, the new day seemed to have
banished them. Her welcoming smile had warmed him
more surely than the exhaust-tinged blast of the Volvo's
heater or the hazy sun that was finally showing through a
break in the fog, and her silent presence so close beside him
now was a subtle torment.

Last night, he'd lain awake for hours in his borrowed
bed, his thoughts moving from Caiti's mute terror on the
rain-damp street to memories of her mouth's caress on his.
Who was she to so disrupt his sleep? He had known her
two days. Just two days. And yet . . .

"A penny for your thoughts," Caiti said.

"A penny's more than they're worth," Griff replied, and
laughed self-consciously when he saw how far he had
driven. "I must have been on auto pilot. If you hadn't said
something, I'd have overshot the target." At the end of the
block, he pulled up beside a parked car in front of Henderson's Café, turned on his emergency flashers and set the

parking brake. "Well, out you get," he said reluctantly. "I promised Nana I'd leave the two of you to eat your brunch in peace, but I'll be back for you in an hour or so."

"You're sure you won't join us?"

Not when the major topic of conversation's bound to be my beard, he reflected, and forced a smile. "Thanks, but I've already eaten."

"You could have a cup of coffee."

"Not this morning," he said. The faint floral scent of her perfume came to him on the still air, a reproach, a temptation. Tucking an errant strand of Caiti's hair into place, Griff sent his fingertip on a gentle downward journey along the rim of her ear. "Knowing Nana's views on frontier justice, I'd better not."

"What do you mean?" she queried, her voice distorted by a shiver—from the morning chill, Griff wondered, or was it a reaction to his touch?

"If I horn in on Nana's brunch, she'll probably invite herself to join us at the museum." Half-lost in the feel of Caiti's skin, he stroked the soft flesh of her earlobe between his thumb and forefinger. "And I don't intend to share you this afternoon, with Nana or anyone else."

A wash of color brightened Caiti's cheeks.

"Better go have your talk," Griff advised, his eyes fixed on her flushed face, "before I decide not to share you at all." He reached across to unlock her door, his pulse quickening as the move closed the final inches between them.

Their eyes met, hers partially veiled by long, pale lashes. The warmth of her breath was a tickling whisper against Griff's skin as he leaned closer still. Her lips looked like satin...felt like satin, sweet to the touch, sweet to the taste, plush pink satin that parted slowly to allow his tongue to stroke the smooth contours of her teeth, and beyond, within, to touch the hot velvet of her tongue, shy and elusive at first, then bolder, rising to meet him, returning his kiss with a sudden passion that seared through his veins.

He heard a car snarl past, and then another.

With a wrenching effort, Griff drew back, drinking in the sight of Caiti's delicate face. "Nana's waiting," he said thickly and cleared his throat. "I guess you'd better go."

"I guess I'd better." She opened the car door slowly and stepped out onto the street. The wind swirled the hem of her drab raincoat, revealing a tantalizing glimpse of pale green skirt and slender legs before she smoothed the material down. "See you in an hour," she promised and closed the car door.

Had he heard another little shiver in her voice, or was it just wishful thinking on his part?

Behind him a horn blared.

Double parked again. With a reluctant wave, Griff put the car in gear and released the brake as Caiti walked away.

CAITI STEPPED from the intimacy of her ride with Griff into the Sunday morning bustle of Henderson's Café, feeling as if she'd crossed the boundary from a fairy tale back into reality. For two days she'd been drifting in a dream, postponing the hard decisions, waiting for the answers to come to her. But it was time, now, to seek those answers for herself.

Nana was waiting for her at a corner table, elegant in a dove-gray dress with a ruche of snowy white lace at the throat. Her silver hair was swept up into a Gibson Girl cloud, her smile serene. "Caitlin!" she greeted her young friend as Caiti joined her at the table. "I've ordered tea and croissants for us, as a start. Would you care for an omelet?"

Caiti hung her coat on the rack and sat down. "Frankly, Nana, I didn't come to eat. I came to see if we could get things straightened out about Griff and the festival." She searched for a place to begin unraveling the tangled thread. "When you recruited Griff for the fund-raiser, why didn't you tell him we wanted him to shave off his beard?"

"Because he wouldn't have agreed to it then."

"Nana, he isn't agreeing to it *now*. Why didn't you warn us, before we sent out all those flyers and got involved with FineArts Radio?"

"Because Griffon wouldn't have believed how successful it could be. I had to let things get far enough along to prove to him what a money-maker this idea was."

In truth, Caiti recalled, Griff had been skeptical of the whole notion. "But I've told him about the money," she reminded Nana. "And he still says he won't cooperate."

"He'll come around."

"'Come around'? When? The festival's less than a week away! I'll have to call FineArts Radio tomorrow and tell them we're canceling."

"No, you can't! You mustn't!"

Caiti spread her hands in exasperation. "What else can we do, Nana? Put if off until we have an auditorium full of people, all waiting for something that isn't going to happen?"

"Griffon won't let us down. You have my assurance on that."

"I can't afford to believe you. I should have canceled on Friday morning, when I first found out he wasn't interested."

"And what would that have gained us?" Nana demanded. "How are we any worse off if we leave matters as they are for the time being? I'm absolutely convinced that Griffon will change his mind, if he just has a few more days to consider the matter. But if you make a public announcement saying that we've canceled, that will put an end to it, once and for all."

"Nana, The Neighborhood's reputation—"

"Will be just as badly damaged by a cancelation now as it would be if we were to wait and cancel at the last minute, next Saturday. And, as to the money..." Nana looked up, brightening. "Ah. Here's our tea."

Caiti waited impatiently while the waiter filled their cups and uncovered the basket of croissants. When she and Nana were alone again, she said, "It makes it worse, in a way, knowing how much money we would have made and all the projects we could have financed. When I think about having to send it all back now..."

"The Neighborhood shall have its money," Nana said firmly.

"What do you mean?"

"I mean that I'll repay The Neighborhood for any contributions it loses, if Griffon *should* decide not to help us."

"But—"

"Do you doubt that I can? Surely you've realized by now that the house where you met Griffon is mine. I'm not without means, Caitlin."

"It's not that I doubt you," Caiti insisted. "But why would you make an offer like that, Nana? I know you've been an active volunteer, but I don't expect anybody to be *that* devoted to The Neighborhood."

Nana looked amused. "My dear Caitlin, what a notion. Certainly I applaud The Neighborhood's good intentions, but I'm offering the money for the same reason I suggested this plan in the first place—for Griffon's sake."

"For Griff's sake?" It didn't make any sense. "I don't understand."

"Nor does Griffon. But it's true all the same."

"But he doesn't want to shave off his beard."

"Yes, dear, I know."

"Nana, you've made promises that put Griff—that put all of us—on a terrible spot."

"Unfortunate but unavoidable, under the circumstances."

"What circumstances? If it isn't for The Neighborhood, why do you care whether Griff shaves off his beard?"

"Because I want him to be happy."

"That's crazy," Caiti contradicted sharply. "You told lies to the fund-raising committee, you committed Griff to doing something he's dead set against, you compromised him with the people he works for . . . all because you want him to be 'happy'?"

Nana nodded.

"I think you'd better explain."

"I'd really rather not," Nana said, suddenly intent on the steam rising from her tea. "It's a private matter, really. A family matter."

Caiti's temper rose. "It may have started out that way. But you've involved The Neighborhood right up to its eyebrows, and that makes it my business, too." Facing Nana's stubborn silence, she said, "I know I can't make you tell me. But I meant it when I said I'd have to phone FineArts Radio first thing tomorrow morning to cancel their involvement in the festival—unless you can give me a pretty good reason not to."

She half expected Nana to respond to her speech with indifference; instead, to Caiti's alarm, the older woman's eyes grew bright with tears. "I'm afraid it won't be easy to explain," Nana said, looking haggard.

"None of this is easy," Caiti said firmly, hardening her heart against the pain in Nana's dark eyes. "But, easy or not, I'd like to hear what you have to say for yourself."

Her demand seemed to hang on the air between them. In all likelihood, no explanation could help The Neighborhood now. But maybe—just maybe—Nana's words would shed some light on the seductive graces and complex shadows that Caiti sensed in Griff. And that, she acknowledged silently, was becoming increasingly important to her. Maybe dangerously so.

Across the table, Nana slipped the billfold out of her purse and unzipped a side compartment.

That's torn it, Caiti thought bleakly. *She's going to pay the bill and walk out.*

But Nana made no move to rise. Instead, she nudged the salt and pepper shakers aside and spread an array of snapshots across the linen tablecloth.

Startled, Caiti leaned forward in her chair to examine them. As always happened when she viewed photographs, one part of her mind stood aloof, assessing the composition and lighting. But that cool appraisal evaporated as she recognized the one subject common to all of the photographs Nana had displayed: Griff.

Caiti bent closer still, intrigued. Here he was as a teenager in tennis whites, and there as a youngster in a school uniform a little too large for him: a color photo revealed the strong jawline his beard now hid, while a dog-eared black and white shot taken years ago showed a delicate, unformed child's face, barely recognizable as the adult whose kisses so dominated her thoughts.

She judged from Griff's appearance that the photographs spanned several decades. There were two people in each shot, and one of them was always Griff, but the others were women—strikingly beautiful young women, never the same one twice.

"I don't understand," Caiti said. "Who are all these ladies?"

Nana pointed to the old black and white snapshot. "This was my daughter, Amelia. Griffon's mother."

The young woman in the picture was lovely, with Nana's dark eyes and high cheekbones, but it was still the image of Griff that drew Caiti's eyes. He stood beside his mother's chair, slender as an elf, his tiny face an enchanting blend of animation and beauty.

"Shortly after that picture was taken, Griffon's father announced that he wanted a divorce, and Amelia—" Nana's hand trembled as she touched the photograph "—Amelia took her own life. Griffon was five."

Caiti stared at her, appalled. "Oh, Nana, I'm so sorry."

Nana waved her sympathy aside. "As to the others, they were Griffon's stepmothers."

"*All* of them?"

"All of them," Nana affirmed grimly. "Colin Falconer took a perverse pride in marrying women for their youth and beauty, and divorced each of them, in turn, before their twenty-fifth birthday. It made Griffon's childhood rather . . . complicated."

Examining the photographs, Caiti read the stiff stoicism that some anonymous photographer had captured on Griff's face in pose after pose, year after year. Only his eyes betrayed him.

"After Amelia's death," Nana said, her voice vibrating with remembered anger, "Colin sent Griffon off to boarding school. I was only allowed to see him for the summers." The lines around her mouth deepened. "And even that was contingent on keeping my criticisms to myself. Not an easy task. When Colin died two years ago, I came as close as I ever have to dancing on someone's grave. He was a charming, handsome, heartless man, and he damaged the lives of everyone who loved him."

Lifting the picture of Griffon and his mother away from the others, Nana slipped it back into her billfold.

"When Griffon was a child, I tried to make our summers together an antidote to the nine months he had to face alone. He had trouble fitting in at school. He was a late bloomer, small for his age, no good at sports and not much better at his studies. But he was bright when he bothered to apply himself. And he had a strong, clear speaking voice and could memorize lines quickly, even then. I'd done a bit of acting in my youth, so I coached Griffon and taught him the few tricks of the trade I knew. The school plays gave him one small way to belong." She sighed. "But it wasn't really enough. Each June, when he came home, I could see what another year away had done to him."

Caiti swallowed against the ache of sympathy in her throat. She knew all too well how long a year could seem when you were alone and unhappy.

Nana gestured at the remaining photographs. "Most of his stepmothers weren't unkind women, but motherhood was the last thing on their minds. In some ways it was worse when Griffon did grow fond of one of them; before long, she was replaced, and he was cast adrift again."

"What about his father?" Caiti asked. "Didn't he care about Griff at all?"

Nana's look was icy. "If he did, he hid it well. Colin Falconer was a talented writer and a successful one, but he acted as if there were only two classes of people in the world—those who were there to wait on him and those who could act as material for his next project. When Griffon failed to fit easily into either category, Colin simply ignored him."

"And what about you?" Caiti prodded, perplexed. "Which category did you fall into?"

Nana smiled crookedly. "For my sins, I was 'material.' Colin's third book was a retrospective of early film stars. An old friend of mine was interviewed for it and suggested that Colin include me. He came to my house for the interview . . . and that was how he met Amelia."

"Wait a minute." Looking across the table at Nana, Caiti squinted, trying to subtract the familiarity, the wrinkles, the distorting sediment of eight decades. "Before, you said you'd done 'a bit of acting.' Are you telling me you were a movie star?"

"A child actress," Nana said dismissively. "I was no more talented than most, but I was pretty, and small for my age, and I had a good, strong voice, like all the Griffons."

Caiti pulled back in confusion. "What do you mean, 'all the Griffons'?"

"Didn't you know? 'Griffon' is my maiden name."

Caiti felt as if a giant light bulb had suddenly snapped on inside her brain. "Of course! You were Little Mary Griffon!" she exclaimed, amazed. "You made all those old pictures with Danny Dunn. You two were the Judy Garland and Mickey Rooney of the early days, weren't you?"

"Hardly," Nana demurred. "We were just a novelty, children imitating adults. If either of us had talent, you'd never know it from those films. And it was all a very long time ago."

But Caiti's thoughts were already circling back to Griff. "That 'old friend' you mentioned," she said, thinking back over Nana's tale, "the one Griff's father interviewed . . . was that Danny Dunn?"

Nana smiled. "Yes. We still see each other fairly often. Of course, he goes by his real name now—Daniel Dunnett."

"The director of the Golden Gate Players!" Caiti said, recognizing the name. Stories within stories, lives within lives....

The people at the next table rose to leave, the scraping of their chairs breaking the spell Nana's words had woven. Caiti looked down at her watch. "Nana, we're running out of time. Griff's going to be back before we know it. I'm grateful to you for telling me about his childhood, really I am, but what does all that have to do with his beard and the fund-raiser?"

"He won't like it," Nana said darkly.

"It's too late to worry about that."

"Yes," Nana admitted, "I suppose it is." She took a sip from her teacup, then said, "I'm convinced that it's important for him to shave off his beard because I know why he grew it in the first place."

"And why was that, Nana?"

"To hide the scars."

Caiti's felt her face go stiff with shock. "Scars?"

"From the accident," Nana said, then sighed when she saw Caiti's blank look. "I'm sorry, my dear. I'm not trying to be obscure; I just don't know quite where to begin. There's so much you don't know about Griffon—"

"I'm beginning to realize that," Caiti said soberly. Did everyone carry some painful secret in his heart, hidden from casual view? For her, it was Angelo's death. For Griff . . .

"It happened when he was in college," Nana said quietly. "He'd bought himself a big black motorcycle, and he rode it up from the campus to be with us for the Christmas holidays. Griffon's father had married Denise that autumn, just a few months before, but he had a publisher's deadline to meet and had taken a suite at the Fairmont, leaving his new bride to fend for herself. Griffon split his time between my house and theirs, trying to get to know her and make her feel at home."

Something in Caiti shrank sadly from the image of Griff, home for the holidays, trying to forge some kind of family feeling between himself and yet another stranger. It must have gotten progressively harder, and seemed progressively odder, as the years went on. The photographs attested to Colin Falconer's taste for younger women, and every marriage inevitably narrowed the gap in age between Griff and each new stepmother.

"But something happened," Nana said, her voice dropping. "A few days after Christmas, I came home from spending the evening with Daniel and found the house dark and locked. When I went upstairs, all Griffon's things were gone. All I found was a note—a scrawl, really. I could barely make it out. It said he'd decided to take his motorcycle and head back to campus a few days early."

"Didn't he say why?" Caiti asked.

Nana's long fingers demolished a croissant, pinch by nervous pinch. "Oh, it gave half a dozen excuses—he was bored, he needed to get ready for classes, he'd promised to help a friend move into a new apartment—but none of them rang true. I suspected that he and Denise had had a falling out, but I could never get either of them to admit to it. Anyway, 'why' isn't important." She brushed the crumbs from her fingertips. "What is important is that he crashed the motorcycle that night, on his way back to the college. The fall broke his right wrist and his collarbone, chipped several teeth, lacerated his face and fractured his jaw."

Caiti winced. "Didn't he have a helmet?"

"He wasn't wearing it. It's a miracle he wasn't killed." Reaching up, Nana toyed with the lace of her collar. "I wasn't notified. The hospital contacted Griffon's father, and he decided there was no point in spoiling my holiday. No point! I ask you!" She looked ready to cry. "Colin didn't even take the time to go down and see for himself how his son was. And so I never knew a thing about it until months later, when Griffon came back for the summer. He sent word that he was flying home, and I went down to the airport to surprise him, but it was I who got the surprise."

"The beard," Caiti said.

Nana nodded. "When I heard what had happened, I begged him to see a plastic surgeon, but he wouldn't even discuss it. He wouldn't talk about the accident at all, except to say that he was fine and I shouldn't worry. Finally I let the matter drop." She sighed. "Perhaps I was even relieved, in a selfish sort of way. Griff had always been a beautiful child. However cowardly it may have been of me, I didn't want to see the damage."

"But now you've changed your mind. Why?"

"Because he's letting it ruin his life," Nana said vehemently. "He finally has a chance at what he's wanted all along, and he's going to pass it up, all because of that damnable beard. Griffon is an actor. An exceptional one. It's what he's wanted to be, what he's worked toward, from the time he was a little boy."

"I still don't see—"

Nana silenced her with an impatient gesture. "Griffon has a decision to make. His contract at FineArts Radio is up for renewal, and the new one they're offering is for several years. He's considering signing it . . . but it would be a terrible mistake."

"How can you be so sure of that?"

Nana scowled. "He belongs on a stage, not behind a microphone. After the accident, he and his father stayed on bad terms, so I wasn't altogether surprised when Griffon went to New York to try his wings. And he's made a grand success of his radio work there. I'll be the first to admit it, to applaud it, even. It was an excellent way to begin. But Colin is dead. Griffon is finally free to come home. If that sounds heartless, I'm sorry, but Colin Falconer made my daughter's life unbearable. The only decent thing to come out of their marriage was Griffon. He's all that I have left of my dear girl, and I'm the only person alive who loves him. I won't see him bury himself at FineArts Radio needlessly. If he stays on there, he'll only stagnate. It's time for him to move on. And he has a chance to do just that. The Golden Gate Players have been holding open auditions," Nana announced with obvious satisfaction, "and Griffon had already made the first cut."

Caiti nodded in sudden comprehension. The Golden Gate Players were a prestigious part of San Francisco's theater community. An invitation to join them would be a major coup for Griff. And, instead of being thousands of miles away in New York, he'd be in San Francisco.

It was a tantalizing thought. A thought to build dreams around.

"He has an excellent chance of being selected," Nana continued. "But a repertory company relies on the versatility of its members, visually as well as vocally. His beard would have to go. Now that they've made that clear to Griff, he's having second thoughts about continuing with the auditions."

The words stung Caiti out of her reverie. "So you set Griff up to shave off his beard because of the auditions?"

"In part. But even the auditions are just a means to an end." Reaching across the table, she clasped Caiti's hand. "It's time that Griffon made peace with himself and came home. Since the accident, he's locked himself away from everyone, out of fear and insecurity. I understood at first.

So much of an actor's self-esteem is bound up in how he perceives himself. The accident was a frightening thing for him to have gone through alone. But that was years ago. The scars may have faded. Even if they haven't, stage makeup can work wonders."

Caiti straightened her spine in exasperated anger. "Stage makeup? While he's performing, you mean. But what about the rest of the time? What about his life?"

Nana smiled. "Caitlin, acting *is* Griffon's life—the most important part of his life. As to the rest, I'm told that cosmetic surgery has made wonderful advances in the past few years." She squeezed Caiti's hand. "But all this is speculation. Griffon doesn't know *what* he has to deal with. In all those years since the accident, he's never once shaved off that beard to find out. And it's high time that he did. But we'll need your help."

Caiti sighed. "What sort of help?"

"I want you to leave things as they are. I don't want you to cancel Griffon's part in the festival. Trust me, Caitlin. More importantly, trust Griffon. He's going to come through for us, if we just have faith in him. I'm sure of it."

She wanted to agree. She wanted to do what was best for Griff. But she had responsibilities to The Neighborhood, as well, and to all the people that The Neighborhood could help. Driven by that sense of responsibility, she asked, "And if he doesn't, Nana? What if you've miscalculated, and he leaves us all holding the bag?"

Nana released her hand. "Then I'm prepared to make good on the money The Neighborhood will lose." Nana's chin rose proudly. "You can count on that, Caitlin. I don't make pledges I'm unable to fulfill. If Griffon refuses to carry through with the festival, I won't be able to mitigate the damage to our reputation, but I'll repay The Neighborhood for the money it loses." She gazed intently into

Caiti's eyes. "It's a gamble. I know that. But for Griffon it's a gamble I'm willing to take . . . if you are. Will you trust me? Will you wait? For Griffon's sake?"

And despite her better judgment, Caiti nodded. "All right. I'll wait. For Griff."

6

A SUBSTANTIAL CROWD had turned out for the Winship retrospective at the San Francisco Museum of Modern Art. Griff followed Caiti from room to room, with their raincoats draped over his arm, viewing paintings that ranged from landscapes to portraits to abstracts: thirty years of an artist's life, captured on canvas.

But a part of Griff's mind refused to focus on the sumptuous colors spread before him. The brunch with Nana had upset Caiti. She could deny it all she liked; her fingers, cold and tense in his, told a different story. She and Nana had probably been arguing about the fund-raiser, but Caiti hadn't said another word to him about it, not a word.

His conscience writhed.

Standing close beside him, she was contemplating a dark landscape illumined by a narrow streak of vermilion along the horizon. Her profile was as pure and self-contained as a child's, but there was nothing childish about the intelligence in her eyes or the soft swell of her breasts and hips. She looked like a flower, straight and still at his side. If he half closed his eyes, her glowing copper curls became petals, rising above the misty green calyx of her dress, the slender stem of her waist. . . .

A fat man pushed closer to the paintings, jostling them.

"Hey, watch where you're stepping!" Griff protested angrily, and pulled Caiti into the safety of his arms. "Are you all right?" he asked her.

"I'm fine." She smiled reassuringly at him and then at the embarrassed man. "Really. It was nothing. Come on, Griff. We haven't seen the still lifes yet."

He let her urge him into the next room, astounded by his own hair-trigger reaction. It had been an accident; the man had meant no harm. But Griff had responded with the same fierce protectiveness he would have shown for Nana or Peggy, filled with a sense of outrage that anyone had dared to threaten the well-being of someone he loved.

Someone he loved.

Griff felt as if he'd stepped from darkness into a sudden dazzle of light, painfully illuminating. That's what Caiti was becoming to him—not a stranger, not someone Nana knew, not a friend, or a date, or a passing flirtation. Somehow, silently, she had stolen into his heart and made a place for herself there.

It had never happened before. He'd never so much as had a crush on the girl next door—there'd never *been* a "girl next door," or even a female teacher, in all those long years of boarding school. Like a frustrated criminal, when he'd had the motive, he'd lacked the opportunity. And by the time he had the opportunity, all the innocent joy had gone out of the chase, and he'd settled for short-term relationships, no strings attached.

Suddenly he wanted strings.

"Look at this one!" Caiti tugged eagerly at his hand. "Isn't it beautiful?"

The still life she praised was barely a foot tall. After the expansive landscapes and dominant abstracts they had already seen, its diminutive size was startling, but Caiti was right: the painting achieved a warmth and dimension that a larger canvas could only have diminished.

Its composition was common still-life fare: two bananas, an orange and a pear rested on a wooden breadboard which, in turn, rested on a wooden table top. In the foreground was an onion; in the background, a blue earthenware pitcher.

It should have been nothing more than an exercise in technique, an emotionless academic study. But the scene was bathed in an intense golden light that cast warm shadows of cinnamon and sable, and the mute objects managed to embody a sense of hearth and home, the familiar made significant, the simple made dear. Studying it, Griff felt a lump of longing form in his throat.

"What's wrong?" Caiti asked, her voice taut with concern.

"Nothing," he denied hastily.

"Not 'nothing,'" she disagreed, her voice quiet in the crowded room. "Something about that painting bothers you. What is it?"

She really seemed to want to know. Griff searched for a way to describe the unexpected emotion twisting through him. "It makes me feel homesick," he admitted impulsively and turned away, appalled at the clumsiness of the word. *Homesick*. It made him sound like a five-year-old at summer camp. Whatever this pain in his chest might be, "homesick" was only one small, misleading corner of it. Even now, with his back to the painting that had started it all, he had to fight an urge to bury his face in his hands and weep bitter tears of pain and loss . . . but for what? What had he lost? What was he mourning? And how could he expect Caiti to understand, when he didn't understand it himself? She must think he'd lost his mind.

Mortified, he turned back to face her . . . and felt his heart unclench in love and relief at what he saw there: the tears he couldn't shed were shining in Caiti's eyes.

BY THE TIME they left the museum, it was raining again. Tightening the belt of her raincoat, Caiti braced herself for a dash to the car, parked several blocks away, but Griff shook his head.

"You wait here where it's dry," he said. "I'll get the car and be right back."

"But—"

"Please? It isn't often I get to be chivalrous."

Stepping back beneath the shelter of the overhang, Caiti watched him go with a sense of wonder. After hours inside the museum, she felt as if a cornucopia of beautiful but conflicting images had been emptied into her mind, a wealth of color and line and image that dazzled her inner eye and left her wishing for the unifying control of her camera. For the span of an afternoon, she herself had been the lens, opened wide to focus with fresh acceptance on each new work of art spread before her.

And through it all, enhancing it, had been the inescapable awareness of Griff's hand in hers, the touch of his fingers at her waist, the occasional warm stir of his breath on her hair.

As she'd walked with him through a maze of art, Caiti's mind had strayed again and again to the little still life that had pushed him beyond his usual smooth control. "It makes me feel homesick," he'd said, turning away from it, and the wistful pain in his voice had awakened an echo of Nana's words: "He's locked himself away from everyone, out of fear and insecurity."

That might well be true. Today she had glimpsed a new side of the vulnerability hidden within him.

But Nana had also claimed, sadly, that she was the only person alive who loved Griffon. And that was becoming less true with each passing hour.

So, the cold voice of reason intruded, *you found out a little about his past. But he's still essentially a stranger to you. And pity's a rotten basis for love.*

Compassion isn't pity, she argued with herself. And there's more to what I'm feeling than that. You know there is. Besides, if I can go on learning as much about him as I have today, he won't be a stranger for long.

That's good, her inner voice observed dryly. *Because you've got less than a week.*

The Volvo's horn sounded, and Caiti ran down the steps and tumbled hastily into the car, as if she could outdistance her troubled thoughts.

"Dodging between the raindrops?" Griff asked with a gentle, teasing smile. He put the car in gear and merged carefully into the late-afternoon traffic. "I know the day's supposed to end now," he said at last, in a tone of wistful entreaty, "but I really don't want to say goodbye yet." Taking his right hand off the steering wheel, he stroked the pulse point of her wrist. "What would you say to dinner for two?"

Regret was a bitter taste in Caiti's mouth. "It sounds wonderful, Griff, but I can't. I'm sorry."

He lifted his hand to the wheel again. "Okay," he said steadily, after a silent moment. "It was just a thought."

The social mask was back in place. Troubled by it, Caiti said, "I don't want the day to be over, either. But this is Sunday, and I always have Sunday dinner with Papa Tony. He's probably been at work in the kitchen since noon. I wouldn't feel right, calling at the last minute to back out."

"Relax, Caiti. It's okay," he said, the intimate timbre of his voice replaced by determined cheerfulness. "Believe me, I understand. After all, I wouldn't want you changing your plans if it was *me* you'd promised to spend the evening with."

An idea blossomed in her mind. Quickly, before she could think better of it, she said, "Come home with me."

"What?"

"Come home and have dinner with us, Griff. I'd like you to."

He shrugged the suggestion away. "I'd better not. It sounds like three would be a crowd."

"You're wrong. Three would be just fine. And with Papa Tony manning the kitchen, there's always enough food for ten. Or maybe twenty." She reached out to touch his arm. "Please? I'd really like you to."

She thought he was going to refuse again. Instead, shooting her a sidelong glance, he said, "On one condition."

"You and your 'conditions,'" she scolded, trying without success to swallow the smile that rose to her lips. "Last night it was 'kisses for photos.' What is it this time?"

"Nothing so entertaining," he admitted. "But if you'll give me a minute, maybe I can think of something better."

Caiti laughed. "First, let's hear your original idea. You'll come to dinner tonight if . . . ? Come on, 'fess up, Falconer. What's the price?"

"Well, Denise is throwing a birthday dinner for Nana on Wednesday night. If you'll come with me to Denise's party, I'll have dinner tonight with you and Mr. Buonarroti. Deal?"

Caiti hesitated. The thought of spending an entire evening in Denise's company was a daunting one. "Won't she object to an extra guest?" Caiti asked.

"Won't Mr. Buonarroti?" Griff countered.

It was a fair question. In all the years she and Papa Tony had been together, she had never brought anyone home to share their Sunday dinner. It would be a public declaration of sorts. Was she ready for that?

Griff stopped for a red light. "Well? Do we have a deal or not?"

There were a hundred good reasons to say no, a thousand, but the word refused to form on Caiti's lips. What chance did reason have when Griff was sitting beside her? He was worth the risk. And trespass into each other's family circle would be one more way to learn who he really was and whether there was any hope for this longing in her heart.

"Deal," Caiti said recklessly, and felt a warm rush of excitement sweep through her as her bridges began to burn.

WITH CAITI ON HIS RIGHT and Antonio Buonarroti on his left, Griff sat at the big butcher-block table that dominated the kitchen, his head bowed while grace was said over the meal.

Even though his eyes were closed and he was sitting motionless, his sense of Caiti's presence warmed him with the subtle persistence of a glowing ember. Since the moment at the museum when he'd realized his love for her, it was as if the outer, public layer of his skin had been peeled away, leaving him naked and new, sensitized only to her. He longed to be alone with her, longed for it in a way he'd never known was possible, eager for the sight of her smile, the sound of her laugh, hungry for the feel of her mouth, her skin, her body beneath his.

"Amen," said the older man, startling him, and Griff allowed himself a guilty smile before he opened his eyes.

When he and Caiti had first come upstairs and through the door that led into the kitchen, the spicy aromas in the air had made his mouth water. Now the sources of those enticing smells were displayed in profusion on the table in front of him: a vast pot of minestrone, steaming tortellini nearly hidden in a cream sauce, a loaf of crusty garlic bread, Cotechino sausage, bowls of crisp radichetta, and the largest pan of lasagna Griff had ever seen.

"What a feast!" he said, overwhelmed. "Where do I start?"

"With whatever's closest," Caiti advised. "But first, a toast."

Griff raised his wineglass obediently and saw Papa Tony do the same.

"To friends of the heart," Caiti said.

The wine was red and robust, warming his tongue as surely as the look in Caiti's eyes was warming his blood. Holding her gaze with his, he took a second sip.

"So," Papa Tony said, "finally I meet the man Caitlin has been spending her Sunday nights with."

Griff choked on his wine.

It took a long, painful minute of coughing into his napkin before the tannin searing his windpipe dissipated. "'Scuse me," he wheezed when he could breathe again.

"Papa Tony didn't mean that quite the way it sounded," Caiti said with a laugh, holding out a glass of water. "He likes to tease me because I listen to 'Heroes & Heartbreakers' every week. Are you all right?"

"I'm fine," he said, and gratefully sipped the water before he turned to smile at Papa Tony. "But from everything I've heard, it sounds more like *you're* the man Caiti spends her Sunday nights with, sir."

As the meal progressed, Griff found his confusion over Caiti's relationship to Papa Tony growing greater and greater. Was he her mentor, as well as her friend and employer? How had they met? Except for their interest in photography, they seemed an unlikely pair . . . and yet the ease with which they interacted spoke of a long and intimate acquaintance. It was obvious that Antonio Buon-

arroti was an important influence in Caiti's life—and that
automatically made him important to Griff.

But the splendid meal made it hard to concentrate on
analyzing the man. After months of restaurant meals and
his own mediocre efforts in the kitchen, Griff found Papa
Tony's cooking a revelation. "I think you missed your
calling," he told the older man, when he had cleaned his
plate and helped himself to seconds. "Even in San Francisco, there'd be room for another Italian restaurant where
the cooking was this good."

Papa Tony passed the lasagna pan to Griff, managing
to look both flattered and offended. "After dinner, I will
show you some of the portraits I have taken of Caitlin.
Then you can decide whether I missed my calling."

"Papa—" Caiti protested.

"I'd enjoy seeing them," Griff assured him, "but no
photograph in the world could compete with your tortellini." He lifted a forkful. "Man eats to survive, but a dish
like this raises survival to an art form."

"And what is photography, if not an art form?"

Great, Falconer. Offend your host. Griff waved the
challenge aside with a conciliatory smile. "If I let you em-
broil me in a debate, my food will get cold."

To his relief, Papa Tony laughed and let the matter drop.

"New topic of conversation," Caiti decreed, and Griff
turned to her gratefully. "You remember the house I told
you about, Papa? That gorgeous old Victorian where I met
Griff? The one I said would be perfect for the Anderson
wedding portraits? Well, I found out at brunch today that
it belongs to Nana."

"You didn't know?" Griff asked in amazement.

Caiti shrugged. "Until today, Nana and I had only seen
each other at meetings for The Neighborhood. She didn't
say anything about who the house belonged to when she

gave me the address and told me to meet you there on Friday morning. I wish I'd known. Has she lived there long?"

"More than sixty years," he said, smiling at the thought. "The house has belonged to the Billingers—my grandfather's side of the family—ever since it was built."

"She must love it," Caiti said softly.

"Absolutely," he assured her. "She says all her best memories are stored there."

"She seems to have kept it in wonderful condition."

Griff nodded. "She babies the place. Over the years, the cost of repairs has been pretty steep, but nothing's too good for it, as far as she's concerned. Last year she put a new roof on it and she completely updated the wiring the year before that. By next year she's going to have to replace most of the old plumbing. One way and another, it's eaten up most of the money my grandfather left her when he died. Some people are 'land poor'—Nana's 'house poor.'" Seeing the stricken look on Caiti's face, he reached out to take her hand. "Don't worry, she isn't going to starve. That house is an investment. It's left her a bit short on liquid assets, but she's got me to back her up now. Denise thinks she ought to sell it and invest the money, but there's no way Nana'd do that. Grandfather Billinger brought her there as a bride. She'd rather pinch pennies in that house than live the high life anywhere else. And I don't blame her a bit. There's a lot of family history there. A lot of memories."

"And the house will be yours someday?" Papa Tony asked. "Or no," he amended. "I was forgetting—Caitlin says that you live in New York City."

Afraid I'm going to talk Caiti into running away to New York with me? Griff wondered with a silent laugh, and found that the thought lingered after the laugh was gone.

"Well, yes, that's where I work, but I still consider San Francisco my home."

"I see. More wine?"

"Please."

Papa Tony refilled Griff's glass. "You have a place of your own here, then? An apartment, perhaps?"

"Not at the moment. When I'm in town, I stay with Nana." What would it be like to have Caiti living with him in New York? What would it be like to wake every morning and find her asleep beside him? It sounded like a hopeless daydream. But sometimes dreams came true. Could he make this one a reality if he wanted it badly enough?

There was a deep line of concern between Papa Tony's bushy eyebrows. "You are here in San Francisco often?"

"Not as often as I'd like," Griff admitted. "The past few years have been a busy time for me. But I grew up in San Francisco, and I'd like to move back here again eventually." He forced a grin. "New York's a wonderful place, but the winters can be hard on a native Californian."

"Yes, I imagine so." Papa Tony folded his napkin and set it on the table beside his empty plate. "Well, I am sure your grandmother misses you when you are away. But Caitlin says that the rest of your family lives here, as well. That must keep her from becoming lonely. Are you enjoying your visit with them?"

"Yes, sir." It was easier to agree than to explain. He didn't want to taint the evening with thoughts of Denise. Pushing back his plate, he went on the offensive to forestall any more of Papa Tony's questions. "Have you always been a photographer, Mr. Buonarroti?"

"Always—first in Italy, then in this fine country. I have had my studio here for more than thirty years now. And for more than twenty of those years Caitlin has been with

me. She first came to me when she was only this high—"
he held his hand out at waist height "—with a little Insta-
matic camera. She told me that she wanted to take pictures like the one in my window of 'the pretty bride.' Do
you remember, Caitlin? 'The pretty bride,' you said, and
Angelo and I—"

"Griff didn't come to hear baby stories about me," Caiti
interrupted. "It's embarrassing."

Griff turned to her in surprise. There was more than
embarrassment in her voice; she sounded deeply distressed. Her cheeks were flushed, and her gaze was fixed
on Papa Tony, silently emphasizing her words.

"Of course," Papa Tony said, abruptly subdued.

An awkward silence fell. Griff searched his mind for a
topic of conversation, however trivial. Anything was
better than the hurt look on Papa Tony's face and the tension he could feel radiating from Caiti. "About Peggy's
pictures," he said at last. "Is there any chance they'll be
ready in time for Nana's birthday party on Wednesday
night?"

Caiti hesitated.

"I developed the film this afternoon," Papa Tony announced.

"Well, then," Caiti said, "I'll print up the proofs tonight
and you can pick out the ones you like tomorrow, Griff.
That should give me time to have the finished portraits
ready."

"I don't want to make you work tonight," Griff protested.

Caiti smiled. "Don't worry, I always do darkroom work
on Sunday nights. It's a habit of mine. In fact, that's when
I listen to your show."

She seemed to have recovered her composure. Griff felt
his own anxiety ease. "Would tomorrow afternoon be

okay, then? Five o'clock or so? I'd like to bring Peggy along
to see the proofs."

"Five o'clock should be all right," Caiti agreed.

"Fine, then," Papa Tony said. "We will see you tomorrow, Mr. Falconer. And now, perhaps you would like
some espresso."

Reluctantly Griff stood up. "Thank you, sir, but I don't
think so. I hate to eat and run, but I should be going soon.
Nana turns in pretty early most evenings, and I promised
I'd be back in time to talk with her awhile before she called
it a night." He gathered his dirty plate and silverware together. "Let me help you clean up."

"No, leave it, please. Tonight you are my guest." Papa
Tony stood up and held his hand out to Griff. "But you will
come again, and the next time you will come as a friend.
Then I will allow you to help."

"I'd like that, sir." Griff accepted Papa Tony's hand-
shake. "And if you ever decide to go into the restaurant
business, remember, I'd be glad to back you. I've been to
every Italian restaurant in New York City, and what I ate
here tonight leaves them all standing at the gate."

"I'll walk you to your car," Caiti offered quietly.

"Déjà vu." Smiling, Griff took her hand, then turned
back to look at Papa Tony. "Do you mind if I steal her
away, sir?"

"Of course I mind." For an instant, the older man's gaze
remained somber; then the twinkle reasserted itself. "But
I will allow it as long as she is back in time to dry the
dishes."

"Then we'd better get started," Griff said and drew Caiti
with him across the kitchen and out the door and down
the darkened stairway that led to the studio.

"The lights . . ." she said when they reached the bottom, but when he pulled her gently closer, she came into his arms with a pliant willingness that took him by surprise.

Holding her, he traced his fingertips slowly up and down the delicate curve of her spine. "I wish I didn't have to go," he murmured, feeling her curls tickle against his lips as he spoke.

"I know," she said softly. "Me, too."

He could feel the warmth of her cheek where it pressed against his shirt, over his heart. "I've been waiting all night for a chance to kiss you."

"I know." She must have tilted her head in the darkness; the whispered breath of her words was a faint flutter against the hollow of his throat. "Me too. But—"

He bent his head and pressed his lips unerringly to hers in the sheltering darkness.

The kiss began as a gentle joining, then flared without warning into something far less controlled. Griff let his hands slide along Caiti's ribs, savoring the outer curve of her breasts and the subtle, enticing flare of her hips beneath his palms. He wanted her to burn for him, to melt with him, to want him even half as badly as he wanted her.

Her hands came up to cup his face, and she drew back slightly, shivering. "Griff—"

He kissed her forehead. "Mmm?"

"Griff—" she repeated, pulling back another step, and he felt her shiver again.

"I'm here." Leaning forward, he kissed her cheek and felt his heart plummet. Raising his fingertips to her face, he traced the little streaks of moisture that ran down her cheeks. "You're crying," he said helplessly, pushing the words past the tightness in his throat. "What is it, Caiti? Tell me." He pulled her to him. "Talk to me," he pleaded, feeling her shoulders shake as she stifled another sob. "Tell me what's wrong."

"I never cry," she said, her voice thick with the tears she was fighting. "Give me a minute."

He gave her a minute, and another, and a third. "Do you want me to go?" he asked then, and waited for her answer while his stomach tightened into an aching knot around the meal he had just finished. When he couldn't wait any longer, he said, "Don't cry, Cait. Please don't cry. Let me help you, whatever it is. I—" *I love you*, he wanted to say, but his throat closed obstinately around the words. Griff took a deep breath. "Caiti, I—"

"I have to tell you something," she said abruptly, her voice sounding strained but steady. "Something I should have told you before I invited you here tonight."

Not sure whether he was relieved or disappointed, Griff put aside his own declaration and gave her the gift of his silent attention.

She laced the fingers of her right hand through his left. "It's about . . . Papa Tony. And me." Her fingers moved nervously in his. "Papa Tony's more than just my boss, Griff. More than just my friend. He's my father-in-law."

Once, playing football when he was in the seventh grade, a ninth grader had knocked the wind out of him. He hadn't thought of it in years, but all the old sensations were suddenly back: the grinding ache beneath his breastbone, the sense of suffocation, the disorientation that kept him from doing or saying anything coherent. . . .

"His son Angelo and I got married when I was twenty-one."

Griff stroked her ringless fingers, remembering his father's string of divorces. Didn't anything last? Didn't people even try to work out their differences, or did they just scrap their marriages at the first sign of trouble? *I love you*, he had tried to say to Caiti, but what did he know about love? The books he read made it sound like some wonderful, exotic blossom, but in reality it was a frail, pitiful thing, a spindly plant blighted by the first hint of frost.

"So," he asked as levelly as he could, "where is he now, this husband of yours?"

"Dead," Caiti said. "He died four years ago."

Griff closed his eyes, feeling sick. "Oh, Caiti, I'm sorry. I'm so sorry." He cradled her in his arms. "I should have known, should have guessed. When you said you didn't date, I thought—I don't know what I thought. But not that."

"I should have told you," she said, "but there wasn't any point at first. I mean, you don't shake some stranger's hand and say, 'Hi, I'm Caitlin Kelly Buonarroti, and I'm a widow.' It didn't have anything to do with meeting you and talking to you about the fund-raiser. And then, when . . . when I got to know you better, I didn't want to tell you. I was afraid it would sound like I was asking for sympathy. And I don't want your sympathy, Griff. So I didn't say anything."

"It's all right," he assured her. "I understand."

"But it isn't all right," she insisted, and Griff could imagine the stubborn tilt of her chin in the darkness. "Not telling you before was my decision. But then I invited you to come here for dinner tonight, and I still didn't explain. And that was wrong and dumb and . . . and selfish of me. It would have hurt Papa Tony if he'd realized you didn't know who he was talking about when he mentioned Angelo, and that hurt would have been my fault. If I didn't want to tell you about his son, I shouldn't have invited you into his home."

"Sounds logical," Griff conceded. "But people don't always act logically. At least I don't." He kissed the top of her head. "You didn't tell me, and you should have. But you salvaged a tricky situation without letting it explode in our faces."

"Barely."

"Hey, in this case, 'barely' is good enough." He hesitated, wishing he could see her face. It was hard to read her reactions in the dark. "Caiti . . . Caiti, I'm glad I was here tonight, and I plan to come back again as often as you'll let me. It might be better if you told me a little more about what happened."

"There isn't much to tell."

"A man is dead before his time," Griff said quietly. "There had to be a reason. What did he die of?"

"An accident," Caiti said, her tone brittle.

"What kind of accident?"

"Hit-and-run."

Griff's mouth went dry. "Last night," he said, "when that car went by. . ." He remembered her panic and the feel of her trembling in his arms. "You said *you'd* been hit by a car. . . ."

Caiti rested her forehead against his chest. "Angelo realized what was happening before I did," she said. Griff strained to catch her words. "He tried to push me out of the way. I got out of it with a concussion and a broken leg. And he. . . he didn't get out of it at all. Internal injuries, they said. He died on the way to the hospital."

"He saved your life," Griff said and felt Caiti nod in silent agreement. The fact that Caiti could so easily have died before he'd ever met her was a fierce pain in his heart, assuaged only by the sweet miracle of her living presence in his arms.

Again, the words *I love you* rose to his lips, but he held them back. This night, this moment, belonged to another man.

Tomorrow would be soon enough to talk to her of love.

7

"OKAY, HERE THEY ARE," Caiti said, trying not to sound smug as she spread the proofs on the table in front of Griff and Peggy. "Just look them over and see what you think."

"It's me!" Peggy said, pointing in excitement.

"They're all you," Griff said, laughing, and Caiti smiled at the fond indulgence in his voice.

"But this one's me and Arthur! That makes it even better. Can we get this one for Nana? Can we? Please?"

"Sure, Peanut. If that's the one you like, that's the one we'll get. But you don't have to decide right away. Take a look at the others, too. What about this one?" he asked, and Caiti saw that he was pointing to her own personal favorite: a profile shot of Peggy, curled up in the window seat, peering out through the rain-spotted glass.

"Arthur isn't in it," Peggy objected.

"Incredible as it may seem, I like it anyway. Besides, it shows off your hair ribbons." He looked up. "What do you think, Caiti?"

Caiti spread her hands in friendly disclaimer. "It's the customer's right to decide. And you two are the customers."

"Coward."

"Absolutely," she agreed. It was past five o'clock, and the studio was closed for the day; ensconced in the little room she and Papa Tony used as an office, she could lean back against the couch cushions with a clear conscience, enjoying the good-natured tone of give-and-take Griff used when he spoke to his little sister.

Last night, as she'd listened to "Heroes & Heartbreakers" while she worked on the proofs in the darkroom, it had been hard to separate her impressions of the "real" Griff Falconer from the sound of his voice on her radio. The sixth episode of *Pride and Prejudice* was airing, and Fitzwilliam Darcy was finally baring his heart to Elizabeth Bennet. "In vain have I struggled," The Voice had declaimed, while images of Griff formed on the sensitive printing paper beneath her fingers. "It will not do. My feelings will not be repressed. You must allow me to tell you how ardently I admire and love you."

It was just a character in a radio play, speaking words that had been written almost two hundred years before, and yet Caiti had felt a little shiver run down her spine. She knew how the story went, of course; Elizabeth Bennet would spurn Darcy's proposal. But eventually...

"Okay, I give up." Griff laughed. "We'll buy both pictures and each of us can give one to Nana. I bet Caiti can find a double frame for them." He turned to her with a smile that spurred her pulse. "Could you do that for us, Caiti?"

"Whatever you like," she said.

"Whatever?" he echoed and, though there was nothing provocative in his tone of voice, the look in his eyes was another matter entirely.

Caiti blushed. "I'll have the eight-by-tens printed and framed by Wednesday afternoon," she said, striving for a businesslike tone as she gathered Peggy's proofs together into a neat pile.

"I knew I could count on you," Griff said, and his gaze supplied a meaning that suddenly made her wish Peggy had stayed home. Reaching past Caiti, Griff tugged gently on one of the little girl's braids. "Well then, Pipsqueak, I guess we're all set. I'll buy some birthday paper and ribbon tomorrow and wrap up the box before Nana's party. Wasn't it nice of Caiti to take your picture?"

"Thank you!" Peggy said, and put her arms around Caiti. "You're nice, and pretty, and I like the picture you took of me and Arthur."

"I'm glad," Caiti said, astonished by the hug. "You and Arthur were very good subjects."

Leaning forward, Peggy looked past Caiti to Griff. "Will Caiti be at Nana's party?"

"You bet," he said promptly. "I invited her yesterday, and she promised that she'd come."

"Can Arthur come, too?"

"Of course," Griff assured her. "It wouldn't be a truly meaningful family gathering without Arthur."

"Will Sidney be there?" Peggy asked, and Caiti saw Griff's smile fade to a look of bewilderment.

"I don't think I know Sidney, sweetheart. Is he a friend of Arthur's?"

Peggy giggled. "Sidney isn't a bear, silly. Sidney's a man. He eats dinner at our house sometimes. Last night he brought me a coloring book."

Caiti saw a look of black anger come into Griff's eyes, but his voice remained bright and casual. "Does Sidney eat breakfast at your house, too, Princess?"

"Griff—" Caiti protested, then bit her tongue. She had no right to interfere. And yet—

"No," Peggy said, to Caiti's relief, then added, "Sidney doesn't like breakfast. But sometimes he watches cartoons with me while he drinks his coffee."

"That's nice," Griff said with ominous calm. "But I don't think Sidney will be coming to the birthday party."

The studio doorbell rang. "Excuse me," Caiti said, relieved by the interruption. "I'll be right back."

Behind her, as she went to the door, she could hear Griff saying, "Let's get our coats and hit the road, shall we, Peg? I promised I'd have you home by six o'clock, but maybe your mom will let you stay at Nana's tonight, instead. Would you and Arthur like that?"

Caiti caught a glimpse of ivory wool as she passed the front window. *Speak of the Devil*, she thought, startled to find Denise Falconer on her doorstep. "Peggy, your mother's here," she called loudly, then unlocked the door and swung it open. "Hello, Mrs. Falconer."

Denise blinked in surprise. "I'm sorry, have we met?" she asked blankly, looking apologetic; then her mouth tightened in annoyance. "Oh, yes. Griffon's friend. Well then, he and Peggy must still be here. I've come for my daughter."

Caiti resisted the temptation to answer rudeness with rudeness. "Yes," she said. "Peggy and Griff are down the hall in the office. Won't you come in?"

"No, thank you. I'm in a hurry."

"Ah, Lady Gracious, Lady Bountiful," Griff said, appearing in the archway. "What an unexpected treat. So kind of you to join us."

"Where's Peggy?"

"Getting her coat. What are you doing here, anyway? I told you I'd have her home by six."

"A change in plans," Denise said shortly.

Caiti looked uneasily from Denise to Griff. The hostility between them was an almost tangible thing, souring the atmosphere of the room like cigar smoke.

"Mama?" Peggy called from the office. "Mama, come see the pictures!"

Denise's gaze never left Griff's. "I don't have time, Peggy. We're going to be late if you don't hurry up."

"Please, Mama? Please?"

"Oh, all *right*," Denise said, and brushed past Griff like a storm front.

"Such a charmer," Griff said dryly, and followed her.

Troubled and embarrassed, Caiti hung back for a long minute, but she heard no more angry voices. Walking warily down the hallway, she found Griff lounging just inside the door while Denise sat on the edge of the couch beside Peggy, sorting the proofs into two piles.

"Some of these are really very nice," Denise was saying. "Tell the photographer I'd like to order a set in four-by-fives, matte finish."

Griff grinned. "If you turn around, you can tell her yourself."

For the second time in five minutes, Caiti found herself the object of Denise's startled scrutiny.

"What's the matter?" Griff baited her. "Cat got your tongue?"

Denise smoothed her hair and focused on Caiti, pointedly ignoring him. "As I said, I'd like to order some prints. When could they be ready?"

"By the first of next week," Caiti replied in a neutral tone. "I'm glad you like them. Peggy was a pleasure to work with. She's a lovely girl. Very photogenic."

"Thank you," Denise said and smiled.

It was the first time Caiti had seen her with a pleasant expression on her face, and it emphasized what she had already grudgingly known: Denise Falconer was beautiful. "Have you ever modeled?" Caiti asked impulsively.

"Professionally, you mean? No."

"Would you consider sitting for me sometime? I'm putting together a portfolio of portraits and I'd like to include you, if you'd be interested."

"I don't know," Denise said cautiously. "I'd have to think about it."

"Please consider it." Caiti took one of the Buonarroti Studio cards from the card holder on the table and held it out to Denise. "Give me a call and we can talk about it."

Denise still looked undecided, but she tucked the card into her wallet before she turned to her daughter again. "All right, Peggy," she said mildly, "stand up and let's get your coat buttoned. We don't want to be late."

With Arthur in hand, Peggy obeyed.

"Hot date tonight?" Griff asked.

Ignoring him, Denise began to fasten the buttons, then stopped, peering at the front of Peggy's dress. "What have you got on yourself?" she demanded.

"Chocolate sauce," Peggy said softly, stealing a look at the offending spot and then at Griff.

Denise turned to scowl at him. "I suppose you've been feeding her ice cream again."

"Guilty as charged," Griff said, looking unrepentant. "*Mea culpa*. Bring on the thumb screws. Better yet, call a policeman and have me arrested. I'm sure Caiti won't mind if you use her phone. Just dial 911."

Denise shot him a withering look as she fastened the final button. "Fine, joke about it. It probably makes you feel good, blowing into town once a year like Santa Claus and spoiling her rotten. But it's no kindness to her." Denise stood up. "I'm sure you two had a wonderful time this afternoon, but someone's going to have to nag her to eat a decent dinner tonight and sit up with her if she gets another stomachache. And who do you suppose that's going to be?"

"Sidney?" Griff suggested.

Denise's head jerked as if he'd slapped her. Taking Peggy's hand in hers, she stalked out of the room.

After a frozen moment, Caiti followed them out.

"Mrs. Falconer—"

"I'll come for the pictures on Monday afternoon," Denise said tightly, and kept on walking, towing Peggy along in her wake.

"The door's locked," Caiti said as they reached the foyer. "Let me get it for you."

Denise stopped, a picture of impatience.

Working the locks, Caiti said, "Mrs. Falconer, Griff has invited me to Nana's birthday dinner."

"Oh?"

Opening the door, Caiti took a deep breath. "It's your party, at your home. I won't come if you'd rather I didn't."

Pausing in the doorway, Denise shook her head. "It makes no difference to me." Her voice had an edge to it, but there was a spark of wry humor in her eyes as she added, "You can sit between Sidney and Griffon, if you like. I may well need a referee."

"I'M SORRY."

Griff said the unfamiliar words out loud to the empty room when he heard Caiti's footsteps returning down the hallway. In her absence, rethinking his confrontation with Denise, he'd reached one inescapable conclusion: he owed Caiti an apology.

When she stepped into his line of vision a minute later, he said again, "I'm sorry."

"For what?" Caiti asked, coming to sit beside him, and the absence of sarcasm in her tone amazed him.

He contemplated the list of his offenses. *I'd like you to think well of me*, he'd told her that first day at Nana's house. Those words were even truer now—and even harder to live up to.

Waiting wasn't going to make his apology any easier. "I'm sorry for airing my family's dirty laundry in front of you," Griff said. "And for putting you on the spot."

"But—"

He held up his hand, and she fell silent. "I'm sorry for pursuing a private argument in a public place," he persisted, determined to say it all. "And for antagonizing a potential customer. And most of all, I'm sorry for showing you again how small and mean I can be when Denise and I start wrangling. That isn't how I want you to think of me. It isn't how I want to spend my time when I'm with you." He looked away, shamed by the calm kindness of her gaze. "And so I'm sorry," he said with difficulty. "Sorry for what happened and sorry for how I acted."

The office was unnaturally quiet. Waiting for Caiti to respond, Griff could hear nothing beyond the shallow rasp of his own troubled breathing.

"Apology accepted," she said, and he felt her fingers ruffle lightly through his hair. "Family arguments are never easy."

"It won't happen again," he promised in relief.

"It may," she disagreed. "I'm sure you and Denise both have your reasons for feeling the way you do. But . . ."

"But what?"

She shook her head. "It's really none of my business."

"Maybe not officially, but you are involved." When she didn't respond, he slipped his arm around her. "I involved you. I hope to go on involving you. And I care about your opinions. Please, Caiti. Tell me what you're thinking." He squeezed her gently to his side. "Come on, camera lady, give me a break. Butt in. Can't you see I'm feeling like a class-A boor? Won't you make even one little faux pas so I'll feel better?"

"Oh, all right," she said, and laughter was a bubbling undertone in her voice. "Just this once, I'll stick my nose in where it doesn't belong. But you'll be disappointed. It's nothing particularly momentous or insightful."

"Let me be the judge of that," he ordered. "Come on, speak your piece."

"All right." She was warm and soft in his arms as she relaxed against him. "You're probably way ahead of me, anyway... but have you thought about how your fights with Denise are making Peggy feel?"

Griff looked down at her, startled, but Caiti's eyes were closed, the lashes visible in a russet curve against the pale contour of her cheek. It should have been enough, having her there in his arms, so near, so trusting, but her words stung his pride. "Of course I've thought about Peggy and how she feels," he insisted. "I'm worried sick about her."

"Oh, Griff, I know you are. You love Peggy. That's obvious to anyone who sees the two of you together. But it isn't exactly what I meant."

"Then I guess I'm being dense," he said, resentment warring with the tenderness he felt for Caiti. "You'd better spell it out for me."

Opening her eyes, she smiled up at him, a smile that melted his defensiveness. "Peggy loves her mother, Griff. She needs to love her mother. But she loves you, too. And when the two of you argue... Well, I saw the look on her face when they left." Caiti sighed. "Peggy didn't say goodbye to me. She didn't even say goodbye to you. I don't think she dared to."

"Dared...? Why wouldn't she dare to?" A horrible thought crept into his mind. "Do you think she's afraid of Denise?"

"No. I think Peggy's confused, maybe even afraid, but not of her mother. From everything I've seen, Denise loves Peggy. And so do you. She's probably what you and Denise fight about most."

It was true. After years of avoidance and suppressed hostility, he was aware that it was his growing concern for Peggy that had drawn him out to do battle with Denise more openly.

"I know you're fighting for what you think is best for Peggy," Caiti said, "but all she sees is the fight itself. Don't you suppose it makes her feel like she has to choose between the two of you? You're her brother, but Denise is her mother. That's an impossible choice for a four-year-old to make, Griff. She's already lost her father. She needs every bit of family she has left. You both do." Her gaze held his for a single, serious moment; then she sat up straighter, pulling away from him, her cheeks flushed. "Now it's my turn to apologize," she said. "End of lecture, I promise."

"Don't apologize," Griff said sadly. "You're probably right." He shook his head, impatient with himself. "No, not 'probably.' You *are* right. It's a mess. We're a mess, Nana and Denise and Peggy and I. If it weren't for Denise—" He stopped himself. "No, that's what I've been doing up to now. Blaming Denise. And it isn't that simple. We try to be a family, and there are lots of two-way connections, but mostly we can't close the third side of the triangle."

"What do you mean?"

"Well, Peggy loves Nana and she loves Denise . . . but there's no love lost between Nana and Denise. Nana and Denise and I are supposed to be the adults in the family, but Denise and I can't agree on the time of day, let alone what's best for Peggy. The only triangle that does work is Nana and Peggy and me . . . and now you're telling me that

shutting Denise out is just another way of hurting Peggy."
The sad futility of it all made him feel old and cold and
very much alone. "Maybe I should just go back to New
York. Nana and Denise might be able to work something
out, for Peggy's sake."

"No, Griff." Caiti's hand was a tentative featherweight
on his arm. "That's no solution. I meant it when I said
Peggy needed all the family she has left. And what about
Nana? She needs you, too."

He could feel the frustration gathering like a weight in
his chest. "So where does that leave me?" he demanded.
"If I stay, I'm hurting Peggy. If I leave, I'm hurting Nana.
What sort of a choice is that?"

"No choice at all," Caiti agreed. "But aren't you turning
your back on another way?"

"What way?"

Her slender fingers stroked slowly up the length of his
arm and down again. "You said Nana and Denise might
be able to work something out, for Peggy's sake. Don't you
think that's possible for you, too? Couldn't you and Denise hammer out some sort of truce?"

"No. I can stay out of her way entirely, but I can't—"

"Reason with her? Work through your differences like
two adults? Why not, Griff? When so much is at stake,
isn't it worth at least a try?"

"You don't understand."

"Maybe you've already tried," Caiti suggested kindly.

"No," he admitted, unwilling to lie, though he knew
how damning the truth must sound to her. "I just can't . . .
Denise isn't . . . You don't understand."

"I know that. Help me. Explain it to me."

The memories made speaking difficult. He didn't want
anything about Denise to touch his time with Caiti. "I
don't want to talk about it."

"I can see that. But maybe it's time you did. What is it that gives you such a low opinion of Denise, Griff? What have you got against her?"

"She's an unfit mother." The words escaped with a venomous intensity that frightened him. Trapping his shaking hands between his knees, he fought to control his anger.

"You really believe that," Caiti said soberly, and he felt her hand come to rest on the nape of his neck. "You must have a reason. What is it, Griff? What has she done?"

"She sleeps around," he said harshly.

"You know that for a fact?"

Griff snorted. "You heard what Peggy was saying. This Sidney must be her latest fling."

"Maybe," Caiti said. "Or we may be jumping to conclusions. According to Nana, Denise has been a widow for over a year, Griff. She has every right to invite a man to dinner."

"And have him stay the night?" he asked in outrage.

"Yes, if that's what happened. It wouldn't be the smartest or the most tactful thing to do, with a child in the house, but it isn't criminal, and Peggy didn't seem upset by it. All she said was that he was there, drinking coffee, while she watched cartoons. Maybe he came over early on a Saturday morning."

"And maybe the tooth fairy will leave a dime under your pillow," Griff said bitterly.

"Maybe so. The point is, you don't know what Denise's relationship is with Sidney. As unlikely as it may sound, it could be proper and aboveboard. And it's not the real point, anyway. You only found out about Sidney today. Whatever you feel about Denise, it goes back a lot further than that." She met his gaze boldly. "Have there been other Sidneys?"

"It wouldn't surprise me."

"We're not talking about surprises. Do you have any real reason to believe that what you said is true? That Denise is promiscuous?"

"She didn't love my father. She married him and she didn't love him."

Caiti leaned forward and kissed his cheek. "Griff, I'm sorry. That's sad, if it's true. But *it* isn't criminal, either. It isn't even uncommon. Do you think he loved her?"

"I don't know," Griff admitted, remembering all the pretty young brides that had come and gone. "Probably not. My father had a weakness for beautiful faces, and an inconvenient habit of marrying what he admired. For a monogamous man, he managed to cut quite a swath. Between attorneys' fees and alimony, the price was steep, but it never seemed to slow him down. He loved them for what they looked like, not for who they were."

"And you're condemning Denise because you don't believe she was in love with a man like that?"

"No. Because she was unfaithful to him."

"While he was alive, you mean?"

"Yes, damn it, while he was alive. She was in someone else's bed within months of the wedding."

"But how could you possibly know—" Caiti looked up at him in distress. "Oh, God, Griff, you walked in on them?"

When he closed his eyes, he could still smell the perfume, see the voluptuous swell of pale flesh in the near-darkness, feel the cool sheets against his overheated body. "It wasn't a question of walking in. It was my bed." The memory forced itself forward, eclipsing everything but the remembered reality of that time and place. "I was home for Christmas. My father was a writer, and he was off on a research trip. Those days he was always off on a research trip. Denise was lonely—hell, they'd been married three months and she'd hardly seen him—so we did things together, the two of us. Went Christmas shopping. Looked at the decorated windows at Gump's and the ornaments at Podesta Baldocchi's. Bought a tree and put it up. Went out to dinner. I showed her around San Francisco. We talked. And then, one night, she cooked for us and I brought wine and we drank it and then we opened some more and drank that, and then . . . we went to bed. Together. And made love. And fell asleep." He drew a wavering breath. "And my father came home unexpectedly, in the middle of the night."

"Oh, Griff—"

His mouth was painfully dry. "By the time I woke up, he was shouting and Denise was crying and . . . well, it got pretty ugly. He threw me out. I deserved it. I stopped at Nana's and packed my stuff and wrote her a note and headed back to campus on my motorcycle, still half-tanked. In a lot of ways, I guess you could say I never went back." Raising his head with an effort, he pulled air into his lungs and pushed it out again, pulled it in and pushed it out, waiting for the queasy ache in his stomach to ease. "Sorry. I'm lousy at confessions." He swallowed. "I never told anybody about that night, till now."

Caiti looked up at him, a slow, pensive look that caused the little lines to deepen around her eyes. "And you and your father . . . ?"

Griff shook his head. "After that, if I came to San Francisco, I stayed with Nana. He never forgave me. But he forgave her."

"Denise, you mean."

He nodded. "At first I told myself to hang on; he'd divorce her in a year or two, like he had all the others, and then maybe I could explain and we could . . . patch things up. But it didn't work out that way."

"And you've never forgiven her for that," Caiti said. Griff looked at her, startled, but she pressed on. "How old was Denise when she married your father?"

"Twenty, I think."

"And how old was he?"

"Well, it was ten years ago, so he must have been . . . forty-five. So what?"

"And you were . . . what? Twenty, too?"

"Almost. What's the point, Caiti? You think it was all my fault and she was the lily-white maiden? Nobody held a gun to her head and forced her to marry my father, any more than they forced her to go to bed with me. So she was lonely. Who isn't? She didn't even know me, not really. She was making love to a face, to a warm body, regardless of who lived inside it, just like my father was doing when he married her."

"They stayed together for the better part of a decade," Caiti said quietly. "They had a daughter, five years into that marriage. Whatever it started out as, maybe it turned into something better. However Denise felt about your father when she married him, maybe those feelings changed. Maybe she even grew up a little. Possible?"

He sighed. "Possible. Anything's possible."

"Maybe Denise isn't the only one you're mad at. Maybe she's just the safest target for all that anger."

He didn't have to ask her what she meant. The answer welled up inside him, overwhelmingly. *He chose her. I was his son, but he chose her, he loved her, he forgave her. And he never forgave me. Never loved me the way I needed to be loved. He spent his whole life making mistakes. I made one, just one, and he never let me forget it. He dumped on*

*me, so I dumped on Denise, and pretty soon she started
dumping back.*

All those years, all that anger... Deep in his heart, in
his soul, he was tired—tired of striving for a forgiveness
that had never come from a man who was dead and gone
now; tired of carrying his anger at Denise like a weight on
his back; just plain tired. It was time to move on. He could
have put the weight down whenever he wanted to; he just
hadn't realized it.

"What a mess," he said, but he could already feel the
worst of the burden lifting. "How do I put Humpty together again, after all this time? Where do I even start?"

"How about Wednesday night? At the birthday party,
maybe you could try just being... noncombative. Don't
throw the first punch. If Denise snipes, bite your tongue
and turn the other cheek. Just for a night. And see how it
goes from there. Think you could try that?" When he hesitated, she said, "For me?"

"For you? Anything." Griff smiled wearily and saw an
echo of his smile brighten her eyes. "I don't suppose my
magnanimous behavior rates a kiss?"

"It might." She took his hand and stood up. "But first
there's something I want to show you. Come on."

All he wanted to do was sleep for a week, but he rose to
join her. "Where are we going?" he asked.

"To the darkroom."

"What for?"

Caiti gestured down at Peggy's proofs. "These aren't the
only pictures I took—or had you forgotten?"

His heart sank. "Actually I was hoping you'd forgotten. Or that the camera had malfunctioned. Or the film
had fogged. Or—"

"No such luck. But I did promise you could see them before anyone else did. Now's your chance. You don't want to forfeit your rights in the matter, do you?"

"Is that a trick question?" Griff asked and followed her reluctantly down the hall to the darkroom. "This looks like the Mad Scientist's laboratory," he said when they were inside.

"Perfectly harmless," Caiti promised. "Although what we can do to a photograph here does seem like magic sometimes."

He watched with uneasy interest as she opened the filing cabinet that stood in the far corner of the room and pulled out a manila folder. "Unfortunately for Nana, these first few shots aren't anything to brag about," she warned, spreading three prints on the counter in front of him. "I've seen mug shots where the subject looked more relaxed."

Looking down at them, Griff laughed in spite of himself. "So I wasn't cut out to be a model. I warned you, didn't I?"

"But the others are something else again . . . although they're no more appropriate for Nana than the first ones were."

"What do you mean?"

"See for yourself," Caiti invited, laying out three more prints.

The sensuality he saw there unnerved him. Was that really his face? His hunger?

Griff stole a sidelong glance at Caiti, but she seemed engrossed in her contemplation of the proofs.

She was right about one thing—they weren't anything he'd give to Nana. The message the camera lens had captured in his eyes was meant for one woman only, and it had nothing to do with the love of a doting grandson.

"This is a man with a serious problem," Griff said, forcing a laugh.

"Oh?" Caiti touched the nearest print with a tentative fingertip. "Did I miss the joke?" she asked, her voice solemn and small. "Were you just proving how good an actor you are?"

"No, I wasn't acting." Reaching down, he rested his fingertip on top of hers. "Can't you read the caption here?"

"What caption?"

"Guess I'll have to read it for you, then," he said, closing his hand around hers. Index finger extended, he pointed out the invisible words. "Right here. See? Clear as a bell: Man Falling in Love."

8

"WHAT?" Caiti asked, afraid to trust her ears.

"Of course, that was two whole days ago," he murmured. "Old news. Two days ago I was still falling. Yesterday I hit ground. Today I'm even starting to get the hang of it."

"The hang of . . . ?"

"Being in love with you." He reached up and pulled the chain on one of the amber safelights. "A little ambience," he said, flicking off the overheads, and came to her, bathed in golden light.

A shimmer of pleasure raced through her as he pressed his lips to the rim of her ear, then to the hollow beneath her cheekbone and the pulse that had begun to beat so frantically just below the curve of her jaw. Feather-light, the touch of his fingers on her cheek coaxed her to turn her head and meet his kiss.

It was the barest touching, an almost accidental brush of his mouth against her own, and then the barest of separations as he lifted his head a breath away. "I love you," he whispered and touched his lips to hers again, gentle as a hummingbird courting an unfamiliar blossom.

Caiti yearned upward, closing her mind to doubt and worry as she answered his kiss with one of her own—not a fleeting, tentative half-kiss, but a fireburst of hope and desire.

She felt Griff hesitate for a startled instant; then his arms came around her, strong and sure. When she tried to pull back from the kiss long enough to tell him what was in her heart, a cry of protest rose from deep in his throat, and she felt his hands tremble as he drew her even closer.

The urgency of their kiss began to spiral out of control. Caiti clung to Griff, aware of nothing but the reality of the man who held her in his arms. Growing light-headed, drowning in the flood of Griff's impassioned response, she wondered if she could master the tidal wave of emotion she had freed in him and in herself. It was a risk she had run once before, and she knew the chance she would be taking. With luck and love and skill, the cresting surge of emotion might carry them safely to shore . . . or it might collapse without warning, separating them forever, tumbling her down to be shattered by its crushing weight—

She pushed the image out of her mind. Later, when she was forced beyond the magic circle of Griff's arms, she would face the world of memories and commitments and fears. Until then, for one brief span of time, she would turn her back on past and future alike and immerse herself in the unexpected wonder of now.

In the minutes that followed, Griff's kiss spoke to her with an eloquence that outmatched even The Voice. As the hot melding of his mouth to hers defined his passion, the journey of his fingertips over her face and throat told her more about his longings and uncertainty than words could ever have revealed.

The taste of him, the scent of him, was intoxicating. When the kiss finally broke, Caiti rested her forehead against Griff's chest for a moment, unable to mask her unsteadiness or the ragged rhythm of her breathing.

Griff's sigh ruffled her hair. "I can't believe what you do to me," he said, his voice quavering artlessly. "Don't let me push you, Cait. Please. I love you. I don't want to do anything you don't enjoy, anything you aren't ready for. . . ."

Linking her hands behind his neck, she tilted her head back and met his eyes, letting him see the smoldering hunger he had awakened in her. "Touch me," she said simply, and found she could measure the impact of her words by the sudden catch in his breath.

In willing obedience, his long, clever fingers began their explorations, following the curve of her mouth, the rise of her chin, the thin, hot flesh of her neck, moving down to trace the delicate twin arches of her collarbones within the open throat of her blouse. Retreating with obvious reluctance from the fevered contact of skin against skin, he stroked the sturdy oxford cloth of her blouse where it covered her breasts.

"Touch *me*," Caiti invited softly.

Even in the safelight's glow, she could see the flush of desire that rose to color Griff's face above his beard. Slowly he raised his fingers to the first button and worked it free; then he turned his attentions to the second button, and the third, and the fourth.

The fifth and final button was out of sight, tucked into her slacks. Watching Griff's hesitation, Caiti waited for him to look up and meet her eyes again. When he did, she nodded, hoping he could see her arousal as clearly as she could see his. The careful delicacy of Griff's attentions was making her feel fragile and precious and strangely, wonderfully new. As he eased the blouse free of the restricting waistband and unfastened the final button, her heart beat faster.

Griff drew a deep, shivering breath.

Caiti looked down. Unbuttoned, the sides of her blouse hung freely, separated by an inch or two, revealing the valley between her breasts and the lace-trimmed silk of her camisole, gleaming against her skin.

Griff bent his head, and Caiti felt him press a fiery kiss to the newly revealed skin just above the lace. Savoring the intimate touch of his lips, she closed her eyes, then opened them again as he turned his attention to the cuff buttons that secured the sleeves at her wrists. When they, too, had fallen free, he raised his hands to the neck of her blouse and slipped the material from her shoulders, coaxing it back until it whispered down her arms.

He caught it as it slid over her nerveless fingertips, and dropped it onto the counter; Caiti watched as it covered the images of Griff she had spread there, masking all the watching eyes except the living ones that caressed her.

Moving silently, he stepped behind her. Caiti found that knowing he was there, so close, seeing but unseen, added a heightened sense of anticipation to nerves that already strained and sang in the half darkness.

At last, the waiting ended as he brushed her hair aside and kissed his way with maddening leisure from the nape of her neck down her spine, inch by searing inch, until he reached the barrier of lace. He lingered there for a moment, then worked his way back up.

When he reached the top, he withdrew, releasing her hair to fall in a tickling cascade across her shoulders.

Caiti stood in the silence, aching for his touch.

When his fingertips slipped suddenly between her heated skin and the thin shoulder straps that secured her camisole, a low moan escaped her. Her breasts tingled, the nipples tightening as she imagined the pleasures to come.

She leaned back, letting her body melt against his, reveling in his strength and the bold evidence of his arousal. She could feel the rapid warmth of his breath against her throat as he teased the straps farther and farther down.

The left strap was the first to fall, followed a minute later by the right, but the silky camisole clung motionless, anchored by the rise of her breasts and the pressure of her back against Griff's body. Caiti's breathing faltered in frustration.

Unhurried, Griff's hands rose to grip her naked shoulders, offering support as he drew slowly away.

At Caiti's next breath, the camisole slithered lower, until its progress was stopped by the thrust of her nipples.

Griff lifted his hands from her shoulders and came to stand in front of her. "You are so beautiful," he said haltingly, the words seeming to escape him against his will. Coming closer, he cupped her face in his hands and kissed her with a thoroughness that left her burning. But instead of repeating the kiss, he pulled back and, with careful precision, lifted each camisole strap back into place.

"Griff—" Caiti protested, stunned, but he smiled down at her with such desire that she fell silent, putting her trust in him.

His fingers wrapped around her wrists, and Caiti relaxed in his hold as he raised her hands to his lips. His mustache brushed the sensitive skin of her palms for an instant as his kiss moved from the pulse in her wrists to the soft flesh in the hollow of her palms, and on to each fingertip in its turn. Then he raised her hands farther, lifting them until her arms were stretched high over her head, her fingers pointing to the ceiling.

Another kiss, deeper and more arousing than before. As it ended, Caiti felt him give her wrists a little squeeze; then he let go. She started to lower her arms, but Griff shook his head in tender denial. Returning his hands to her wrists, he drew her arms taut again before releasing them.

Caiti's pulse skipped as she sensed his intention. Holding the pose he had set for her, she met his next kiss eagerly, swallowing a whimper of excitement as she felt him grasp the hem of her camisole.

Griff's fingers traced briefly over her navel; then he slid his hands to either side, over the tensed muscles of her abdomen, and tightened his hold on the slippery silk.

The kiss tapered away, leaving her panting. *Hurry*, she wanted to cry as she felt the camisole's incremental ascent, and yet she knew that each slow-motion movement stoked the blaze that Griff had kindled within her.

Surrendering herself to Griff's sensuous assault, she waited impatiently for the next descent of his mouth to hers. Instead, he sent the tip of his tongue to explore the whorls and caverns of her ear, and Caiti found herself undone by the wrenching delight of his caress. Her senses swam as the tension of her upstretched arms fed the shivery pleasure dancing through her veins.

"Please," she whispered.

He answered, "Yes," but Caiti was unsure what it was she wanted or what he had promised her. The backs of his fingers climbed from rib to rib as the camisole reached the lower swell of her breasts, hesitated there for one tortured breath and them moved inexorably upward, gliding over her aching nipples.

Something like a sob tore from her throat, and Griff was quick to soothe the sound away with a kiss. Caiti welcomed it, although the blend of comfort and torment brought on by his kiss only intensified the raging need that was shaking her. For minute upon minute, she knew nothing beyond the elemental blending of Griff's mouth against hers, and she fought against his attempt to bring the kiss to a close until she realized that there was a new sensation against the cords of her throat: the cool, sleek glide of silk. The camisole was at her chin, ready to be removed.

Caiti let her head fall back, achingly aware that each breath she took brought her breasts in fleeting contact with

Griff. From the rhythm of his breathing, she knew that he was just as aware of the contact as she was.

The lacy camisole tickled against her lips as Griff began to draw it over her head. For a long moment, she was enclosed in it, seeing the amber glow diffused through its folds, feeling it flutter as she exhaled. Then her mouth was free to meet Griff's again, and the safelight was shining into her eyes, bright by comparison with its momentary eclipse.

Griff guided the silk over the points of her elbows, over her arched wrists, over her reaching fingertips and off.

As she lowered her arms, his kiss began to migrate, from her mouth to her chin, from her chin to her throat, from her throat to the upper curve of her right breast. As Caiti rested her hands on his shoulders, he knelt in front of her and flicked his tongue back and forth across the pulsing tip.

Shaking, she laced her fingers through Griff's hair, unable to resist touching him. He cupped the fullness of her breasts, his thumbs flirting over the eager peaks with tantalizing dexterity. "Please," she whispered again, barely recognizing the voice as her own, and Griff swayed forward and closed his lips around one throbbing nipple while his fingers attentively courted the other.

Caiti writhed in his grasp, lost in the devastating magic of his hands and mouth. It was too much. It could never be enough. She was falling, soaring, quivering as jolts of pleasure rocketed through her, each tremor stronger than the one before.

Griff found the button at the side of her waistband and freed it, moving on to tease the zipper slowly down its track. Gently his hand slid beneath the scanty barrier of silk that remained, down through the warm, hidden curls, descending until his fingertips discovered her and began an intimate exploration.

She was beyond the point where she could even wish to call a halt to the exquisite storm he was creating in her blood. At each stroke of his tongue, each caress of his fingers, there was an answering surge within her, a melting glory that built and built until suddenly it burst, shimmering through her veins like quicksilver.

She was no untried virgin. She had known pleasure and fulfillment in her husband's arms . . . but it had been a mellower sensation, the final destination at the end of a long, patiently traveled road, not this precipitous wellspring of delirium that Griff had tapped in her. When the flaring pulses of ecstasy began to ebb, allowing the return of coherent thought, Caiti found herself sitting on the floor, half on Griff's lap, half off, with the fingers of one hand tangled tightly in his hair and the other clenched in his shirtfront, her breath still coming in gasping sobs.

He was holding her, murmuring in her ear, stroking the damp skin of her back in a slow, lulling pattern. When Caiti eased the grip of her cramping fingers, he kissed her temple and then her mouth. There was love in his touch, and tenderness, but his kisses and the rhythm of his hand against her skin were designed to soothe, not incite, despite the unresolved tension of his body beneath hers. When a shiver shook her, he pulled the blouse down from the counter and draped it around her shoulders.

"Griff . . ." she faltered.

"Hmm?"

"I . . ." She ducked her head, grateful for the dim lighting. "Thank you. I'm sorry. I didn't—"

"Hush." He coaxed her chin up and kissed her again, a kiss that spoke of both arousal and restraint. "Everything's fine. Relax."

"But you—"

"Stop worrying. What just happened was beautiful. If nothing else, it did wonders for my ego." His smile of re-assurance deepened into a theatrical leer. "Besides, the evening's young. Would you care to see my etchings?"

"You're a crazy man," Caiti accused him, suppressing a smile.

Slipping a hand beneath the unbuttoned blouse, Griff spanned her breast with the warm arch of his fingers, nestling the nipple into his palm. "Does that mean yes?"

"Caitlin?"

It was Papa Tony's voice, muffled by distance and the walls and doors that intervened.

Before Caiti could react, Griff had scrambled from beneath her and taken a stand, facing the closed door of the darkroom, screening her from the view of anyone who might come in.

Touched by his protectiveness, Caiti climbed to her feet and hugged him. "Thank you, you're sweet, but it's all right. Don't worry."

"Caitlin?" came Papa Tony's call again, and they heard the heavy rhythm of his feet descending the stairs.

"All right!" Griff twisted to stare at her in consternation. "Get dressed!"

"I will. But he won't open the door. When you turned the safelight on, it triggered a red warning light out in the hall." She tried not to smile at Griff's look of dawning comprehension and relief. "He won't come in while the warning light is on, I promise."

Papa Tony's footsteps sounded in the hallway. "Caitlin?"

Caiti slipped her arms into the sleeves of her blouse, more for Griff's peace of mind than her own, and stepped closer to the door. "In the darkroom, Papa. Is something wrong?"

"That Mrs. Hanson from The Neighborhood just called, looking for you."

She stared at the door in surprise. "Did she say why?"

"She said there was a meeting about the festival. She wondered if you needed a ride."

The meeting. Dear God, she'd forgotten all about it. "What time is it, Papa?"

"Half past six."

Caiti's heart plummeted. Half past six. And the city-wide organizational meeting for the festival was due to begin at seven. "I . . . I lost track of the time," she admitted.

Papa Tony chuckled. "It is easy to do, in the darkroom. Is there anything you need me to finish for you?"

"No, that's all right," Caiti said, unable to resist smiling impishly up at Griff. "I'll be out in just a few minutes. But thank you."

"Well, then, have a good time," he said. "I will go back and finish my dinner."

As his footsteps faded back down the hallway, Caiti turned to face Griff. "I'm sorry, I don't want to go, but—"

He forestalled her apology with a wave of his hand. "I'm already enough of a thorn in The Neighborhood's side without making you play hooky, too." He lifted her camisole from the counter. "In fact, I've been thinking about that. About the whole festival, really."

A little bubble of hope began to form in Caiti's chest. "You have?"

He nodded, walking to her. "It isn't fair for you to lose all that money. No matter how you look at it, you and The Neighborhood are innocent parties, caught in the middle between what I'm unwilling to do and the promises that

FineArts and Nana made." Unbuttoning the three buttons she had fastened, he slid her blouse off. "And it *is* a good cause." Leaning down, he kissed her breasts gently, then cocked his finger, pointing an imaginary gun at her ribs as he drawled, "Reach for the sky, varmint. This here's a hold-up."

Caiti raised her arms. "So what's the solution? The festival's on Saturday."

"The solution," Griff said, as he guided the camisole over her head, "is a compromise—I give a little, they give a little."

"Fine. But who gives what?"

"Well, think about it." Griff smoothed the fragile lingerie into place with loving care. "What the people who'll be there really want is to see the man from 'Heroes & Heartbreakers.' What the people who mailed donations really want is a tangible souvenir of their generosity, in this case a lock of my hair. And what *I* really want—" he sent the faint ridge of his fingernails skating up and down over the silk that covered her sensitive nipples "—is to retain my privacy. So we meet halfway and do our best to appease everybody."

"How?" Caiti asked bluntly, determined not to be sidetracked by the dizzying ripples of pleasure Griff's fingers were creating.

"I'll come to the festival, do a reading and let your tame barber cut my hair and trim my beard. That way, you'll have locks of my hair to send to people, just like you promised. The ones who are actually there may have some grounds for complaint, but they'll be getting a live reading in compensation. And if you have to refund some of their money, I'll guarantee to repay that amount to The Neighborhood within a year. It solves everything, doesn't it?"

"I don't know." She took a step back. "I don't think so."

"Why not?" he asked, looking surprised and defensive. "I thought it was a pretty good all-round solution, myself. What doesn't sound fair to you? Who loses out?"

"Everybody, in a way."

"That's ridiculous! If some little old lady in Rhode Island sends The Neighborhood ten dollars, and she gets a lock of my hair, why shouldn't she be perfectly satisfied?"

Lifting her blouse out of his hands, Caiti shrugged into it. "It's hard to explain, Griff. I don't think you really understand what it is about this that caught people's imaginations and got them so involved." She sighed. "I don't think it's something you want to understand."

"What's that supposed to mean?"

Bending her head, she focused on the buttons as she fastened them, encasing her body in a protective sheath of clothing, away from the tempting delights of Griff's touch. "The thing that kindled all the excitement," she said carefully, "the thing that got all those people to sit down and address an envelope and send us their money, was the mystery of it."

"The mystery of what?" he asked, sounding aggrieved.

"Of the unseen." Caiti searched her mind for an analogy he could accept. "Raising the curtain. Unveiling the statue. Tearing away the cat burglar's mask. Most of those people don't care about getting a lock of your hair in the mail. What they want is to find out what you really look like under that beard, and to know that they played a part in getting you to shave it off."

Griff looked desperate. "What difference does it make to them? I'm not the only man in radio who wears a beard. Why single me out? Why are they making such a big deal of it?"

"Because *you* made such a big deal out of it. First you caught the public's attention with your resistance to publicity, then you held it with your talent. You built a mystique around yourself, one that the romantic overtones of the show reinforced."

"But I didn't mean to!"

She wanted to cry—for Griff, for herself, for The Neighborhood's quandary. "I know you didn't. But that's what happened." Tucking in her shirttail, she said, "I'm not turning down your compromise. I just think you need to know what people's reactions are apt to be before you promise to cover the refunds we have to make. There may be a lot more of them than you're planning on."

"You could be wrong," he said shakily.

"I could be."

"But you don't think you are."

"No." She touched his beard, thinking of the scars that Nana said lurked beneath it. "Think it over. Tomorrow you can let me know if your offer still stands. Right now, though, I have to run or I'm going to have thirty soggy volunteers waiting at the school for me to unlock the door and let them in."

"Caiti, the offer—"

She placed a finger on his lips. "Take tonight and think it through again, Griff. Please. Whatever choice you make, be sure it's a decision you can live with." She traced the line of his mouth, then dropped her hand to her side. "Call me tomorrow?"

He nodded. "I'll be out most of the day, but the evening's free. Could I interest you in a night on the town?"

Caiti smiled. "You could probably interest me in sandstorm insurance."

"Six o'clock?"

"Make it six-thirty and you're on."

"Six-thirty it is. Twenty-four long hours from now." Griff reached for the light switch. "Ready to face the real world again?"

Caiti sighed. The real world. The world of memories and commitments and fears. However sweet it had been to shelter in each other's arms, Griff was still at the mercy of his secrets, and she was still committed to her responsibilities. They had begun to forge a sense of trust and connection, but it was too fragile, as yet, to bridge the gap between them.

"Ready," Caiti said, and shielded her eyes as the unsparing illumination of the overheads came on.

9

"'SHE'S DEAD!'" Griff strode across the stage, full of grief and rage. "'I've not waited for you to learn that. Put your handkerchief away—don't snivel before me. Damn you all! She wants none of *your* tears!'"

Nana cowered for a moment in the face of his wrath, then lifted her chin with stubborn pride and faced him down. "'Yes, she's dead! Gone to heaven, I hope; where we may, every one, join her, if we take due warning and leave our evil ways to follow good!'"

The scene was from *Wuthering Heights*, and their voices reached Caiti clearly where she sat, enthralled, in the last row of seats.

The night before, driving to the festival's organizational meeting with her body still glowing from Griff's attentions, Caiti had expected to find Nana there. Instead a note was waiting for her, inviting her to join Nana at noon the next day, if she could possibly get free.

Despite the inconvenience, it hadn't occurred to Caiti to refuse. She needed to see the older woman, face-to-face, to find out whether the "resources" Nana had spoken of so blithely in her promise to help The Neighborhood actually meant the beautiful old Victorian she called home. It didn't matter how desperate The Neighborhood's financial condition might become; Nana couldn't be allowed to sell the roof from over her head.

And so, a little before noon, Caiti had followed the directions given in the note, expecting to arrive at a res-

taurant. Instead she found herself negotiating traffic in the
theater district. When she finally found a parking place
and walked to the address in the note, Nana was waiting
impatiently for her outside the old brick building that
housed the Golden Gate Players. "Just slip into a seat in
the back row," she'd counseled Caiti. "You're in for a real
treat—unless they find out I've brought you, in which case
they'll probably toss you out on your ear."

"They?"

"The audition committee. Quiet now. Not a sound!"

A few minutes later, as Caiti's eyes were adjusting to the
darkness, Griff and Nana stepped into view on the well-
lit stage. Something in Griff's stance had drawn Caiti's eye
in that first moment, a magnetic sense of presence that held
the thread of her attention as surely as if he had closed his
fist around it. She already knew what he could do with
The Voice; now she witnessed his other skills, and learned,
beyond a doubt, that her instinct at their first meeting had
been right: he belonged on the stage.

In the twenty minutes following his first entrance, Griff
had already performed a pair of brief scenes, first speaking as a gifted, half-illiterate Welsh coal miner, while Nana
portrayed the spinster schoolmarm determined to free the
gift of his intellect in a scene from *The Corn Is Green*, then
in the role of Jack, with Nana as the formidable Lady
Bracknell from *The Importance of Being Earnest*. Now
they had changed personae again, and the mood was
darker as Catherine Earnshaw's servant, Nelly, broke the
news of her mistress's death to Heathcliffe.

"'Did *she* take due warning, then?'" Griff was demanding, and Caiti winced at the bitterness that overlaid his
grief. "'Did she die like a saint? Come, give me a true history of the event. How did—'" For an instant, as he tried

to speak his dead love's name, his anguish was visible; then he pushed ahead sternly. "'How did she die?'"

"'Quietly as a lamb!'" Nana averred. "'She drew a sigh, and stretched herself, like a child reviving, and sinking again to sleep; and five minutes after I felt one little pulse at her heart, and nothing more.'"

"'And—did she ever mention me?'" Griff asked, the tremor of vulnerability in his voice wringing Caiti's heart. The stage was bare of scenery; the lighting was flat and harsh; Griff's corduroy slacks and brown pullover were casual and contemporary. . . and yet none of it mattered. Each word, each gesture told her firmly that he was Heathcliffe, and that the heart hidden beneath his stony manner was being torn apart.

"'Her senses never returned.'" Nana smiled at him pityingly. "'Her life closed in a gentle dream—may she wake as kindly in the other world!'"

At her words, Griff's features were transformed by a black fury that chilled Caiti's blood. "'May she wake in torment!'" he cursed. "'Why, she's a liar to the end! Where is she? Not *there*—not in heaven—not perished—where?'" His gaze searched the stage feverishly, and it was clear, when he spoke again, that his words were addressed to the newly freed soul of his beloved Cathy. "'Oh, you said you cared nothing for my sufferings! And I pray one prayer— I repeat it till my tongue stiffens—Catherine Earnshaw, may you not rest as long as I am living! You said I killed you—haunt me, then! The murdered *do* haunt their murderers, I believe. I know that ghosts *have* wandered on earth. Be with me always—take any form—drive me mad! only *do* not leave me in this abyss, where I cannot find you! Oh, God! it is unutterable! I *cannot* live without my life! I *cannot* live without my soul!'"

He fell to his knees, his anguish echoing slowly into silence.

Caiti swallowed against the lump in her throat.

"Fine, fine," a voice said, breaking the spell, and Griff rose to his feet as a spry little man climbed onto the stage and came to shake his hand. "That should do us nicely. Thank you, Mr. Falconer."

A small group of men and women—the audition committee, Caiti surmised—rose from their seats near the front of the theater and filed out through a door beside the stage. When they were gone, the white-haired man patted Griff's shoulder. "Thank you for coming down again on such short notice. The committee has narrowed the field, but they didn't feel right about making a decision before they'd seen the finalists one more time. We should be able to let you know our decision by Friday."

"Mr. Dunnett—" Griff said, as the little man started to turn away. Caiti sat up straighter in her seat. So that was Daniel Dunnett, founder of the Golden Gate Players!

"Yes, Griffon?"

"It's only fair to tell you that I'm still not sure I—"

"Don't put the cart before the horse," Daniel Dunnett admonished. "You've got some very stiff competition. Wait and see whether the committee selects you. Then you can decide whether it's a position you'll accept. No point in theorizing ahead of your data, eh?" He laughed, drawing a smile from Griff. "Besides, auditions like this keep you on your toes. You can get soft, doing everything on tape delay. It never hurts to stretch your craft. Am I right?"

"Yes, sir," Griff admitted.

"Of course he's right," Nana said firmly, and kissed Daniel Dunnett on the cheek.

"Attempting to sway the judging?" he teased. "On your way, Marion. I've promised your grandson a glimpse of our upcoming season schedule. This way, Griffon. We really do have a few surprises up our sleeve for next year..." They vanished into the wings, leaving Nana behind.

Realizing that they were finally alone in the theater, Caiti went down to join her.

"Well, I only flubbed my lines once," Nana said in greeting, and accepted Caiti's help in negotiating the steps at the edge of the stage. "Not bad for an old actress past her prime. And Griffon! Wasn't he magnificent?"

"Wonderful," Caiti said whole-heartedly. "You were both wonderful."

As they walked up the aisle, Nana looked back over her shoulder and smiled at the stage with impish glee. "The others will have their work cut out for them, if *I'm* any judge of talent. I know I'm not being objective, but how can I be? The boy is something special."

"Yes," Caiti agreed, "he is."

Nana's smile widened. "In your objective opinion?"

"In my decidedly biased opinion," Caiti admitted as they stepped out into the sunlight. "Come on," she invited. "We can dissect the whole performance over lunch."

Nana looked surprised, then amused. "Actually, dear, I already have a lunch date, and I'm going to be late for it if I don't hurry." Raising her hand, she hailed a passing cab.

"But I need to talk to you!" Caiti protested.

"Later, dear. I know it's rude to invite you and then leave so abruptly, but I didn't think you'd want to miss the audition."

Watching the cab pull away, Caiti realized that Nana was right: the audition was something she'd needed to witness. In some strange way she couldn't define, it had acted as a lens for her, focusing her doubts and emotions into a sudden clear conviction: she loved Griffon Falconer, in all his talented, tormented complexity. And, whatever the risks, she was going to do her best to make him a part of her life.

GRIFF WAS FLYING. He knew, distantly, that his mood was an aftereffect of a successful audition—a surge of adrenaline—but the explanation couldn't dim his enjoyment of the heady result. All afternoon he'd wandered the city, too keyed up to go home, counting the hours until he could be with Caiti. And now he was.

Across the table from him, lovely in a dress of some silky ivory fabric, she was pursuing an elusive sliver of *sashimi*. As if she sensed his gaze, she looked up and smiled ruefully. "If God had meant for man to pick up raw fish with chopsticks, he would never have invented forks and fingers."

"Allow me." He captured the offending morsel and raised his chopsticks to offer it to her. "Open..." he prompted, wishing that her lips were closing around his fingers, not two undeserving sticks of wood "...and close." The memory of her mouth beneath his was more potent than the steaming *sake* in his cup. And the look in her eyes said that she was remembering, too. "Tasty?" he asked, when she swallowed suddenly.

Her expression wavered between embarrassment and invitation. "Delicious," she said softly, and he felt his pulse jump. "Where did you learn to be so deft?"

"It's all in the wrist," he told her with a smile.

He had brought her to dine at Origami, a Japanese restaurant that rose above its noisy location on Van Ness Avenue to create an oasis of tranquillity and culinary delight. The brightly lit sushi bar had suited him well enough on previous visits, but tonight called for a more intimate setting. He and Caiti shared a little booth, lit by colored lanterns, shielded on three sides by paper screens. They sat on a traditional *tatami* spread over the floor, their feet tucked into a hidden well beneath the table. "Not authentic," he had laughed, "but a nice concession to Western inflexibility."

When a young girl in an elaborately embroidered kimono had cleared away the appetizers, she set platters of tempura and teriyaki and a huge bowl of steamed rice on the table between them. Then, with a measured bow, she backed away and drew the fourth paper wall into place, ensuring their privacy.

It was what Griff had been waiting for. All afternoon, his anticipation had been building toward the moment when he could be alone with Caiti and share his news with her. *I did something important today. I was nervous, but I did it anyway, and I think I did it well.* That was the essence of what he wanted to tell her, the sense of accomplishment he wanted to share.

But sharing was something he had never been very good at, and he found a hundred unexpected insecurities rising to stand between the impulse and the action. She wouldn't understand. Or she'd think he was just demanding her abstract admiration. What was he supposed to say? *You didn't see it, but take my word for it, I was great.* The Ego That Devoured San Francisco.

And so he found himself postponing the decision from minute to minute, filling the silence with small talk and flirtations until, to his chagrin, their plates were empty, and the bill was paid, and they were in the Volvo again, driving through the night streets.

"That was fantastic," Caiti said, sounding relaxed and replete. "Thank you for everything."

He wished he felt as satisfied. At the audition, he had taken a dare and won. Now another, less obvious gauntlet had been thrown down, and he was leery of accepting the challenge. The temptation to confide in Caiti was strong, but so was his conviction of the pain she could cause him with a careless word, a skeptical look, a polite response.

When he stopped the car along a vacant stretch of curb marked Bus Stop, just down the block from the studio, Caiti turned in her seat to look at him. "Come up for a cup of coffee."

Looking at her, Griff sensed that they had reached a crossroad. For the first time, she was asking him into her home, into her private life. It wasn't an invitation to be accepted lightly. He loved Caiti. He'd told her so. But where were those words now? What good would his emotions do either of them if he was afraid to trust her with his hopes and fears?

He'd seen the sterile fate of his father's marriages, based on nothing but a physical attraction. It took hearts and minds to build a real relationship. If he wasn't willing to confide in Caiti, he might as well say goodbye and walk away from her while he still could. *Fish or cut bait, Falconer. Either you're in or you're out.*

Put that way, the choice was no choice at all. He killed the engine. "A cup of coffee sounds great."

The cool night air steadied him on the short walk from the car to the studio. Nerves, he reasoned, were something an actor learned to come to terms with, a balancing act on the cutting edge. If you were too keyed up, you might blow a performance; not keyed up enough, the performance would be flat. There were tricks of the trade, ways to transform the mind's distress before it could betray the body, ways to escape that intrusive sense of self so that you could slip inside a character's skin, see through his eyes, speak with his mouth.

But this is life, he told himself, *the real thing.* And the tension flooded back.

In the archway, Caiti was juggling keys, turning off the alarm, unlocking the door, switching on lights, relocking the door as he followed her in. With his hand in hers, she led him through the reception area, past the stairway, past the studio where they had traded kisses for photos, past the office where he and Peggy had looked at proofs, past the darkroom where he had held Caiti in his arms, all the way to the end of the narrow hallway, where a closed door barred their path.

The Inner Sanctum, the voice in his head intoned as Caiti used her keys.

"Let me get the lights," she said, stepping in ahead of him, and Griff hung back in the hallway, with no idea what sort of room he expected to see when the lights came on.

A lamp came to life in the darkness, and then another.

"Come on in," he heard her say.

He crossed the threshold and felt his eyes widen in surprise.

The room was a gallery, decorated—furnished—with photographs. Huge black-and-white prints dominated the one long unbroken wall; smaller constellations of photographs covered the remaining vertical stretches, mostly black-and-white, the occasional color prints gleaming like gemstones.

"Take off your coat." She stepped toward an inner hallway. "Maybe you'd like to put some music on while I go and start the coffee."

Mechanically he did as she requested, shrugging out of his jacket and tuning the stereo receiver to a station that could be relied on to supply smoky jazz in the evening hours. But his attention was on the four walls that surrounded him.

It was a room of a thousand faces, old and young, watchful and carefree. A celebration of humanity. As intimidating as he found the unexpected sea of faces, Griff soon became aware of an underlying sweetness and strength in them, a connecting thread of joy and beauty that had nothing to do with physical perfection.

And one face was familiar.

Drawn against his will, he walked to the far well and found his own image peering intently back at him, life-size, mounted at eye level.

It was like facing his alter ego, a self who had somehow earned a place here in Caiti's rooms, in her life, wearing his adoration of her like a banner for all the world to see.

"Griff?" The sound of Caiti's voice jerked him around to face her, feeling as guilty as if he'd been caught reading her mail. "The coffee's on," she said. "I'll be with you in just a minute, all right?"

He nodded numbly, and she vanished around the corner.

Left alone again, he surveyed the room with fresh eyes and found it less bare than it had first seemed. The center of the hardwood floor was covered by a large oatmeal-colored rug, woven in the complex, raised patterns he associated with Irish fishermen's sweaters. A long, low sofa in charcoal gray ran half the length of one wall, flanked by small glass tables, and a larger, multileveled glass table against the opposite wall held the components of the stereo system. Fat cushions, large enough to sit on, were piled in one corner, a drift of black and tan against the pale gray wall.

But the faces that adorned the walls were the room's focal point. It was the furniture, not the photographs, that seemed incidental. With anyone else he might assume that the pictures were "wall art," a bold way of decorating an apartment. With Caiti, he never doubted that she had taken and printed each picture herself, and could tell, if asked, who each person was, and what private dreams had floated through their minds as her shutter snapped.

Griff fought back a sense of inadequacy as he looked at the people who lived on Caiti's walls and thought about the fascination they held for her. Was there room, in that broad, impersonal passion of hers for humanity, for a more private alliance?

There had been, at one time in her life, or she wouldn't have married. He knew her husband's death had been a blow, but had it turned her affections exclusively outward, to embrace a world she could capture on film and hold forever, a world that could never leave, never fail her?

"Man falling in love," he had said to her, but she had had no words of love to speak to him in return.

"Cream or sugar?"

Even the timbre of her voice was becoming precious to him. "Black," he said, going to her, and a fierce resolve woke in him: if she didn't love him, she'd have to tell him so. Until she did, he'd do everything he could to win her. To be worthy of winning her. And if that meant being vulnerable, he would do his best to open himself to her.

Taking the mug she offered, he waited while she settled herself at one end of the sofa, then sat down beside her. "I didn't expect to see myself on your wall," he said.

Caiti sipped at her coffee, avoiding his gaze. "Life is full of surprises."

He wanted to ask her why she had hung his picture there, but he reminded himself that his resolve was to open himself to her, not to force her to confide in him. Not yet.

He raised the mug to his lips and took a cautious swallow, letting the bite of the steaming coffee brace him. The intimacy of sitting in Caiti's apartment, alone with her, made him wish he could abandon the words he lived by and escape from the images that ruled Caiti's life. In silence, in darkness, his body could teach hers of his love for her. But he wanted more than that. He wanted so much more.

Taking his courage in his hands, he said, "Bet you can't guess what I did with my day."

Caiti cocked her head, her expression contemplative. "Do you really want me to guess?"

Last chance to back out, Falconer... "Sure," he said and almost winced at the forced nonchalance of his tone.

She set her cup on the end table. "Then give me your hand."

He stared at her. "My hand? Why?"

She smiled. "If you want me to guess, you'll have to let me see your hand."

"Which one?" he asked, bewildered by her request.

"The right. Here—give me your cup."

He handed it to her, waiting tensely while she set it beside her own.

"Now give me your hand."

He extended it.

Caiti took his right hand between both of her own and tilted it, exposing the palm.

"What are you doing?"

"I'm Irish," she said and smiled again.

"So?"

She looked up at him. "Does the word *fey* mean anything to you?" she asked and, without waiting for an answer, bent low over his hand. A moment later he felt the warm puff of her breath against the hollow of his palm, and then the tickling touch of her fingertips, tracing the lines graven in his flesh.

"I see a dark place," she said, her voice low, "and a bright, bright light. One face and many voices." Again, she leaned down to send a warm breath of air across his skin, then returned to her scrutiny. "Emotions, dancing in the air like sunbeams and lightning." She lifted his hand, cupping it gently to her cheek. "I see a great talent," she said, meeting his eyes, "and a small figure sitting far away in the darkness, laughing, crying, afraid to applaud and too moved to leave."

It was an effort to swallow. "You were there," he said wonderingly, both threatened and freed by the realization.

She nodded. "Nana brought me." Taking a deep breath, she said, "Griff, it was like nothing I've ever seen, like stepping through a doorway and watching a piece of someone else's life up there on that stage. Where did you learn to do that?" Her gaze was intense. "Do you have any idea how good you were today?"

Embarrassed, he shook his head. "I don't think there's a safe answer to that question. Sort of a variant on 'Have you stopped beating your wife?'" Somehow, knowing that she had seen his performance and approved of it was enough; he didn't need to hear any more. "Acting is what I do. I mean, when I'm doing it well, that's when I feel that I'm really me, really being what I can be. I was . . . pleased with the way the audition went. And I'm glad you were there to see it. Let's leave it at that, okay?"

"All right, have it your way," she said gently as she studied his face. "But you're an odd duck, Griffon Falconer."

He laughed, startled. "Is that good or bad?"

Her fingers tightened reassuringly around his. "Come a little closer and I'll show you."

The coffee he'd sipped might as well have been brandy from the way his head was spinning. Drawn by the glow in Caiti's green eyes, he leaned toward her. "Close enough?" he asked, when only an inch of air separated his mouth from hers.

"No."

He passed his lips over hers, a whisper of contact. "Close enough?" he asked, feeling his mouth graze her skin as he spoke.

Her eyes closed. "No."

Griff kissed her with tender restraint, enchanted by the game, the tension, the implicit promise of her actions. Her mouth was warm and pliant beneath his. He touched the tip of his tongue to her lips and felt them begin to part. "Close enough?" he asked, the words muffled against her.

She shook her head in denial, letting her mouth brush back and forth against his.

Cradling her face in his hands, he deepened the kiss. As it intensified, he began to lose his sense of the game, his sense of time, his sense of self. Nothing could be sweeter than the willing communion of Caiti's mouth on his—or so he thought until he felt her fingers moving over the muscles of his back, following the length of his spine from shirt collar to belt, tracing the curve of his ribs from back to front, rising to press against the pounding of his heart, moving with precision down the buttons of his shirt until her cool fingertips could steal inside and stroke his fevered flesh.

His own hands began to rove, drifting down to the dainty swell of her breasts, each just filling his hand, as if by design. The material of her dress was thin and smooth, the bodice an unbroken expanse that denied him access even as it revealed the excited rise of her nipples.

Under Caiti's ministrations, the tails of his shirt pulled free of his slacks. Griff suspended the kiss and drew a gulping breath, searching her gaze. "Close enough?" he demanded, the words rasping dryly in his throat.

Her fingernails scraped delicately over his bared chest, making his nipples rise. "No," Caiti said with soft insistence. Taking his hand in her own, she raised it to the zipper at the nape of her neck. "Closer."

With shaking fingers, he gripped the zipper tab and eased it down inch by inch, then slid the dress forward, over her shoulders and down her arms, until the bodice lay in a shimmering pool at her waist.

He had been expecting to see a camisole beneath it, but tonight she wore a bra, an airy froth of satin and lace that stole away what little breath he had left.

"Closer," Caiti murmured.

With her help, he gathered the folds of the dress and lifted it off over her head, draping it hurriedly over the back of the couch. Then he dragged his shirt off and turned back to her—but the driving sense of urgency that rippled through him at the sight of Caiti half-clothed, her lips still damp from his kisses, made him hesitate. He wanted to share a blend of poetry and passion with her, an act of love, a memory to be cherished, not an impulsive mistake she might regret.

"Griff?" Caiti questioned with soft concern.

Wishing his hands were steadier, he lifted the dress and handed it to her. "Here. You'd better put this back on."

"Back on?" Caiti froze. "Why?" she asked, her voice wavering uncertainly. "Griff, what's wrong? I thought…" She made no move to take the dress from him. "I don't understand," she said, and he could feel the intensity of her gaze as she searched his face. "You said you loved me. I thought you wanted this as much as I did."

The pain and confusion in her voice was all his fault. "I *do* love you," Griff assured her, cursing his awkwardness. "You're the best thing that's ever happened to me. I couldn't stop loving you even if I tried—any more than I can stop myself from wanting you."

"Then I don't understand," she repeated in a whisper.

"I'm sorry, sweet Cait, it's so stupid, but I . . . I wasn't expecting you to ask me in tonight. I wasn't expecting to have a chance to hold you, to kiss you, to touch you. . . ." He fought to control his breathing and find the words to explain. "I want you, I want you more than I can say—but I can't protect you."

Her brow furrowed for a moment; then she smiled. "Griff, it's all right."

"No." It was all he could manage not to take her at her word and join himself to her, but he resisted the madness in his blood, intent on doing what was right. "I won't put you at risk like that. I won't."

"But, Griff, it's—"

"I love you," he said, willing her to hear the truth of his words. "I want to go on holding you, kissing you—but I think you'd better put your dress back on first."

"Griff, listen to me." She kissed him, smothering his protests. "I meant what I said. It's all *right*." With her cheek pressed to his, she said softly, "You say you want me. Well, I want you, too. I'm glad you care enough to want to keep me safe, but you don't have to worry about 'risks.' Not tonight. After I made the coffee, I excused myself because I was hoping this might happen. You don't have to worry about protecting me. I've already taken care of it."

The silence that followed her words was broken by the bittersweet strains of Duke Ellington's "Sophisticated

Lady." Griff could feel the sick anxiety draining away, supplanted by a sweeter tension. *I want you, too,* she had said, and his pulse danced in response. She wanted him, wanted him enough to have taken her own precautions. For a second time he draped her dress over the couch back. "Excuse me, miss," he said, smiling into her eyes. "May I have this dance?"

The look Caiti gave him was a heavy-lidded entice-ment. "I think that could be arranged."

He stood and offered his hand. Accepting it, she un-folded from her place on the couch with graceful eager-ness. In her stocking feet, dressed in her bra and a silky half slip, she seemed tiny beside him, a fragile object to be handled with infinite care.

He tried to take her in his arms, but she held back. "You're seriously overdressed," she admonished, as her slender fingers unfastened his belt and slid it free. "Club regulations are perfectly clear—no outer garments are to be worn on the dance floor. And you'll have to remove your shoes, sir."

"Of course," he said, trying to keep his voice steady in spite of what her hands were doing to him. He stripped off his loafers and socks and kicked them to one side. "I for-got. How foolish of me. Would you—" his voice snagged in his throat for a moment as her hand moved to the zip-per of his slacks "—like some assistance?"

"I think I can manage," she said coolly, but there was nothing cool about the gentle intimacy of her fingers as she slid the zipper down and released it, letting the slacks fall around his ankles. "Would you care to hang those up?"

"No." Stepping out of his abandoned clothing, wearing nothing but his briefs, he opened his arms to her. "I'd care to dance with you."

She came to him without further demur, rubbing her cheek against his chest as they began to move to the music.

The air was chilly against his exposed skin, and Caiti was a miracle of warmth in his arms. He held her tightly, reveling in the subtle thrust of her breasts against his ribs and the cool glide of her half slip against his thighs. In that moment, life seemed wonderful to him, something to be cherished, a fine thing that would soon be even better.

On the radio, "Sophisticated Lady" gave way to a dreamy rendition of "I Didn't Know About You." Smiling, Griff kissed the top of Caiti's head, where her hair glinted copper in the lamplight. "Close enough?" he asked, for the sheer pleasure of hearing her reply.

"Closer," she whispered against his heartbeat.

Obedient to the hunger they shared, he explored the clasp of her bra with eager fingertips. When it opened, he drew it back and smoothed the straps from her shoulders, down her arms and off, watching, entranced, as her breasts were revealed. He cupped them in his hands, stroking the nipples with his thumbs in tender greeting, delighting in the way they stiffened and rose at his touch, like exotic buds awakening from a frozen winter. "Bloom for me," he breathed, as their color deepened to dusky rose.

When he felt a tremor wash over Caiti, he tried to capture her mouth with his, but she melted out of his grasp, sinking slowly to the floor, her fingers trailing down his sides, over his hips, down the length of his thighs and up again.

When she reached the barrier of his briefs, it was Griff's turn to tremble. He groaned hoarsely as she slipped one hand between his legs, tantalizing him with the fleeting delicacy of her touch as she explored and then withdrew.

"You're destroying me," he gasped with a helpless, breathless laugh.

"You taught me how." Her fingers slid just beneath the edges of the hot, restricting cotton and came to rest on the pulse points that thundered at either side of his groin. "Close enough?" she asked.

He had to swallow before he could speak. "It isn't fair," he told her huskily.

Her fingers slid upward, so near, so near to where he wanted them to be. "What isn't fair?"

It was getting harder to follow a line of thought and force the words out. Griff wet his dry lips. "*You're* the one who's overdressed now," he insisted raggedly. "You must be wearing three times as much as I am."

Her fingers retreated, leaving a trail of devastated nerve endings in their wake. "So?"

He forced a stern tone. "So decide which two-thirds you're ready to drop."

She smiled up at him saucily. "Or else . . . ?"

Her teasing touch had left him throbbing. "Or else I'll have to decide for you."

Her dimples flickered briefly. "I suppose fair *is* fair." She got to her feet. "How long do I have to make up my mind?"

"About ten seconds. If you're lucky."

"All right." Stepping back away from him, she began to raise the back hem of her half slip. Watching, Griff realized that she was accomplishing the move with a blend of enticing skill and absolute discretion that would have done justice to Gypsy Rose Lee. With a graceful wriggle, she managed to start the panty hose on their descent without allowing him more than a glimpse of her upper thighs. Slowly the hem of her slip lowered into place as she pushed the panty hose down and stepped out of them. "There," she said, straightening with a flourish. "Now we're even. Ready to dance again?"

"Oh, no you don't. That's only one."

"No," she said mildly, and Griff felt his heart slam against his ribs as she reached into the discarded hosiery and produced a pair of light blue panties, like a magician pulling a rabbit from his hat, "actually, that's two."

He closed his eyes, hardly daring to envision what was—and wasn't—beneath that wisp of slip. "I swear, Caitlin Kelly, you're going to be the death of me."

"Not anytime soon, I hope." The throaty, intimate note in her voice was a clear incitement to riot.

He opened his eyes, hoping she could see the maelstrom she created in him, hoping she knew what power there was in her slightest word or touch. "What are you doing way over there, all alone," he asked in wonder, "when you could be here, in my arms, where you belong?" He took a step toward her, trying to read her gaze, trying to make her read his. "I love you, Caiti. I want you. I need you. And if you don't take pity on me soon, I swear I'm going to shatter into a million pieces."

And then she was in his arms, and her mouth was on his, and the sweet agony was everywhere. When he could stand it no longer, Griff bent and lifted her into his arms.

"What a charlatan," she scolded, her voice thick with passion as she clung to him. He carried her down the hallway, searching in the near darkness until he found her bedroom. "You said we were going to dance together."

"We are," he vowed, and lowered her onto the bed. It only took a moment to remove her rumpled slip and another to step out of his briefs, and then he was beside her, learning her body with his hands, coaxing, stroking, until she granted his questing fingers access to her deepest secrets and sweetest mysteries.

Her hands were as greedy as his own, darting over his skin, wringing cry after cry of pleasure from him as she grew bolder, until it seemed to Griff that she was everywhere at once, wrapping him in a golden web of sensation.

With infinite care, he wooed her onward, guiding her closer to the flame. At his urging, Caiti rose to her knees and leaned over him, letting the tips of her breasts brush across his lips. He was attentive to first one, then the other, drowning in desire, savoring each new sign of her arousal. She had been a thing of pure beauty last night when she'd surrendered to her body's pleasure in his arms, and he wanted nothing less for her tonight.

Despite the darkness, it seemed to Griff that the room was awash with color, as if, somewhere just beyond the edge of his vision, a tapestry were being assembled, its fire and complexity intensifying with each unsteady breath he drew. When Caiti sank down beside him and welcomed his body into her own, he felt that he was opening himself to her, as well—encompassing her, drawing her deeper and deeper into his heart, his soul, his life.

Suddenly he felt her convulse in a long shudder of ecstasy that shattered his last semblance of control. The fragmented colors surged, raging through him in a cascade of sharp, high peaks that possessed him completely before fading to a trembling whisper, a throaty echo, a satisfied sigh.

Peace.

Peace and contentment.

A swell of protective longing unlike anything Griff had ever felt prompted him to enfold Caiti in his arms. With his fingers tangled in her hair, he pressed his lips to her love-damp skin in a drowsy, sated kiss, savoring the miracle of her presence as he slipped with her, by slow degrees, into sleep.

10

WHEN CAITI AWOKE, she was disoriented and alone.

The alarm clock's luminous hands claimed it was five minutes to eleven. Eleven at night, she reasoned dimly. Why was she awake? What...?

As her memory clicked into gear, Caiti let the amazing events of the day tumble through her mind: the audition, dinner at the Japanese restaurant, her pretense at palm reading, dancing to "Sophisticated Lady"...and, through it all, Griff. Unbelievably, unregrettably, Griff, in her arms, in her bed, her shadowy dream lover turned to satisfying flesh and blood. The last thing she could remember was the tender strength of his arms enfolding her as she fell asleep.

Reaching out, she found a ghost of warmth still lingering in the rumpled sheets.

"Griff?" she called softly.

No reply. Was he gone? Had he slipped away into the night without a word?

Caiti turned the bedside lamp on, squinting as it lit the room. As her eyes adjusted, she spotted a pair of briefs on the bedroom floor and smiled. Griff could have left without them, but it hardly seemed likely.

But where was he? And why?

Pulling on her robe, she went in search of him.

The bathroom door stood open, the tiled room beyond it chill and empty. She knotted the belt of her robe with nervous fingers and stepped out into the hallway, moving toward the light.

In the living room, the lamps were still on, and her spirits lifted, but there was nothing to be found but the trail of their abandoned clothing and Griff's framed face gazing at her from the wall. She picked his slacks up off the floor, folding them neatly over the back of the couch beside his shirt, wondering what had driven him from her bed.

The only room left was the kitchen. As Caiti walked toward it, her bare feet moving silently on the cold floor, she caught the faint scent of coffee on the air.

From the doorway she could see Griff, dimly illumined by the light from the living room, standing with his back to her as he gazed out of the night-black window.

"Griff?"

He turned at the sound of her voice.

"Are you all right?" she asked, half afraid to hear his answer.

"All right?" He laughed huskily as he came to her and took her in his arms. "I'm on top of the world."

Relieved, Caiti surrendered herself to the reassuring warmth of his lips on hers.

"And you?" he asked with concern when the kiss tapered to an end. "Are you all right?"

"Couldn't be better," she promised, her courage returning. She traced her fingertips along his spine, savoring the little shiver of response that ran through him. "But if we're both doing so well, why are we in a cold kitchen instead of a warm bed?"

"My fault," Griff acknowledged. "I woke up a while ago and couldn't get back to sleep, so I gave up and reheated what was left of the coffee. I didn't think you'd mind."

"Of course I don't mind. You're welcome to my left-over coffee anytime you want it. But caffeine in the middle of the night is hardly a cure for insomnia."

"True," he conceded. "But I'm not planning to go back to sleep. Not yet, anyway. Not here."

All Caiti's insecurities flooded back. "Oh," she said, not trusting her voice beyond a monosyllable.

"No, not 'oh,'" Griff said with a smile in his voice. "If I had my way, you and I would be in bed together right this minute, and we'd damn well stay there until somebody sent a search party in after us."

Yes, the voice inside her cried, *stay with me. Stay!*

"But I can't," he continued. "At least, not tonight. I'm Nana's houseguest, and I've got a courtesy curfew."

Caiti peered up at him, perplexed. "A what?"

"Sounds silly, I know, but it's an understanding Nana and I have. I'm welcome to stay out all night, if that's what I want to do, but she assumes I'll be home by midnight unless I call before she goes to bed and tell her otherwise. I meant to call her, but she turns in around nine, most nights, and at nine o'clock the woman on my mind was definitely not my grandmother."

"I can't very well complain about that," Caiti said, pressing her warmth greedily against his sleek-muscled nakedness. "I wanted your undivided attention."

"And you had it. Oh, Cait, I wish I could stay. Chances are she'll sleep the night through and never miss me. But a phone call in what she calls 'the middle of the night' would scare her half to death. And if she woke up and I wasn't there, that would worry her, too."

Remembering Nana's tale of the night when Griff had failed to come home and all had not been well, Caiti said nothing. However much she wanted him to stay, she knew he would have to leave before midnight.

"So," he went on, "I was planning to finish my coffee and then decide whether to wake you up and say goodbye or leave you a note and call you first thing in the morning."

Caiti shivered at the thought of waking to nothing but a note, then shivered again as the night chill crept beneath her robe. "I'm cold," she said. "And if I'm cold, you must be freezing, standing there in nothing but your smile. Didn't anybody ever warn you against running around at night without your clothes on?"

"Of course. Pajamas were mandatory at every boarding school I ever went to, and I haven't worn a pair since. What's the matter? Is the sight of all this male pulchritude more than you can take?"

"Oh, finish your coffee," she scolded, grinning. "I'm going back to bed before frostbite sets in."

"No, we'll both go." Taking her hand, he walked with her back to the brightly lit living room. "As unlikely as it may seem, I prefer your company to warmed-over coffee. Of course, if it had been fresh brewed...."

She laughed and groped for a fitting riposte, but the sight of him in the lamplight emptied the words from her mind. She longed to capture him on film as she saw him in that moment, unself-consciously naked, unself-consciously beautiful. He was finer-boned than Angelo, pale instead of swarthy, the patterns of auburn hair on his body a subtler contrast to his skin than Angelo's raven curls had been. Griff looked like some artist's conception of twenty-first-century man, stream-lined and stylized, less physically powerful than the man who had shared her marriage bed, but just as desirable.

Reaching to gather his clothes from the back of the couch, Griff hesitated, smiling at her. "Is my tie crooked?"

"Was I staring?" Caiti blushed, struggling against a sweet tide of desire. "I'm sorry."

Coming closer, he toyed with the belt of her robe. "Are you? I'm not. You can look all you want to." His fingers negotiated the hasty knot she had tied. "Just tell me one thing. Do you like what you see?"

She nodded.

"Well, so do I, pretty lady." The ends of the knotted belt came free in his hands, and Caiti's robe slid open. "Believe me," he said, encompassing her waist with gentle hands, "so do I."

When he leaned forward, she met his lips willingly, letting the kiss escalate from invitation to demand. By the time he lifted his mouth from hers, Caiti's skin was glowing with warmth. "But you have to go home," she whispered with reluctance, already half lost in the magic of his touch.

"I know," he said unsteadily. "I will. Soon." His arms closed around her in fierce possession. "But not yet. Not quite yet."

She leaned into his strength, treasuring the moment, willing it to last. There was no room for uncertainty, no room for doubts or fears. There was only the absolute conviction that she and Griff belonged together, and that the moment, although it seemed too beautiful to bear, was only a prelude of the joy to come.

When he finally released her, it was only to lift his hands and smooth the robe from her shoulders, revealing her as fully as he was revealed. Any lingering shyness Caiti felt at standing naked in the lamplight was counteracted by the heady excitement of Griff's touch.

"Caiti . . . Caitlin . . . beautiful Cait . . ." He stroked the smooth skin of her back, pressing her closer against the hard warmth of his desire. "You're a madness in me, a fever burning bright, so bright—" his lips drifted down the line of her throat, stopping for a moment to nibble at her collarbone "—sweet delirium—" then dipping lower to bestow a spangle of kisses across her breasts, his beard caressing her sensitized skin. "Promise me," he murmured and ran the tip of his tongue over one eager nipple.

"Anything."

"Promise me there isn't any cure."

Charmed, she tried to laugh, but he drew the tip of her breast into his mouth with an insistence that caught the laugh in her throat and changed it to a moan of pleasure.

With an answering moan, Griff intensified his loving assault, his hands creating patterns of delight as he explored her body with a bold delicacy that left her gasping. Transfixed, Caiti closed her eyes, tracing his cleanboned features with her fingertips as if love had deprived her of sight.

When the ripples of arousal Griff created within her threatened to surge out of control, she knelt to capture his mouth with her own again. "Love me," she entreated brokenly. "Please, Griff...." Another tremor raced through her. "Love me ... come to me ... make love to me...."

"Your wish is—"

Caiti watched the rest of the phrase die on his lips as her impatient fingers slid down to claim what was rightfully hers.

It was intoxicating to wield such power over him. Enchanted, she whispered, "At a loss for words, Mr. Falconer?" and threw her arms around him, tumbling him with her to the carpet.

They rolled for a moment like children at play, first Griff on top, then Caiti, then Griff again, but the moment was too charged for the game to go on for long. Reveling in the pressure of his lean body against hers, Caiti wrapped her legs around him, capturing her captor. Then, shifting the final necessary inch, she let out a shuddering breath of delight as she felt him slip into her, defining her, completing her.

He was hard and sleek and hot, as hungry for her as she was for him. With driving urgency, she searched with him until they found the rhythm that compelled them. Surrendering to it, they surged together, higher, harder, faster, joined in glorious pursuit, until the sudden moment when there was no air to breathe, no light to see, only an overpowering blaze of sensation that wrung a long cry of exultation from Caiti and then, before the sound could fade from the air, a hoarse echo of it from Griff.

AT TEN THE NEXT MORNING the roses arrived—three dozen peach-colored blossoms whose heady scent drifted up from the nest of green paper inside the florist's box.

Enchanted, she opened the card tucked among them and read the words printed there. "All night have the roses heard/ The flute, violin, bassoon;/ All night has the casement jessamine stirred/ To the dancers dancing in tune..."

Tennyson, Caiti reflected, smiling. She bent her cheek to the satin petals. "You said we were going to dance together," she had teased Griff, from the safety of his embrace. "We are," he'd answered. And they had, in a dance as old as time, as sweet and fleeting as a dream. It had been a night of astonishing joy, a disarming blend of hunger and humor, patience and passion.

Before she'd met Griff, the thought of making love to anyone but Angelo had been impossible. What would she do without the unspoken understandings she and Angelo shared? Would another man find her as desirable as he had? What if her new partner were too aggressive? What if the caresses Angelo had found exciting seemed dull or offensive to someone else? What if, what if, what if—

But in Griff's arms she had discovered a new truth: nothing was more arousing then learning to please and be pleased, if a context of loving trust had been established. When Griff had finally left for home, a scant ten minutes before midnight, it was as if he had taken all her doubts and insecurities away with him. She had fallen asleep in a golden haze, and that same sense of well-being greeted her when she awoke. Even the twinges of her body when she rose had been welcome reminders of the night's loving excesses.

Shortly before noon Caiti completed the second photo session of the morning: four-year-old twins, an impatient father with a lunch date pending, a mother who was afraid that smiling would accentuate her double chin, and the largest Doberman pinscher Caiti had ever seen.

"Congratulations," Papa Tony said when they were finally gone. "You seem to have survived untouched."

"Not quite. I got my finger bitten." Seeing Papa Tony's horrified expression, she laughed. "By the two-year-old, Papa, not the dog."

"Well then, it sounds to me as if you have earned a reward." He held out a small cardboard box. "A messenger delivered this for you a few minutes ago. I hope it is something pleasant."

Caiti untied the string and lifted the lid, not sure what to expect. Inside, she found a card. "Your chariot will arrive at seven," it read. "Wear the green dress again. Please." Burrowing beneath a deep layer of cotton, she discovered an exquisitely detailed brass figure, scarcely an inch tall, with the body of a lion and the head and wings of an eagle.

"Very nice," Papa Tony said, "but what is it?"

"Can't you tell?" Caiti smiled, balancing the little figure on her palm. "It's a griffon."

"WAIT," GRIFF DEMANDED and transferred the telephone receiver to his left shoulder while he fumbled in the desk drawer for something to write with. "Could you read that to me again, please?"

The Western Union operator obliged him, her voice calm and disinterested. "'Griff. Photographers and full video crew set for Saturday. Local media alerted. Fine-Arts brass delighted. See you Monday. Break a leg. Jack.'" She cleared her throat. "Will you want a printed copy, as well, sir?"

"Yes. Thank you."

Damn Jack Sherwood and his high-handed publicity stunts. Griff broke the connection and consulted his watch. Two minutes to two; that made it two minutes to five in New York. He dialed quickly, hoping for the best.

After the seventh ring, a softly feminine voice said, "FineArts Radio. Will you hold?"

"Sue? Have a heart. This is Griffon. I need—"

"Griffon! How was Hawaii?"

He made a face. "Tropical."

"What?"

"Fine. It was fine. Sue, I'm trying to track Jack Sherwood down. Could you see if he's in?"

"Sure. Hang on."

There was a moment of silence, followed by a recorded description of upcoming FineArts programs—another of Jack's bright ideas. "... conclusion of our Mozart Festival, followed by Nigel Thames with 'The Week in Theater.' And remember, on Saturday, in San Francisco—"

Griff's mouth went dry.

"Griffon Falconer of 'Heroes & Heartbreakers' will be shaving off his beard to help raise funds for—"

The recording cut abruptly, replaced by Sue's apologetic voice. "Griffon? Are you still there?"

Yelling at Sue wasn't going to solve anything. "I'm here," he said grimly.

"I found Dinah, but she says Jack's already gone for the day. Did you want to leave a message?"

He could think of several, none of them fit for polite company. "Tell Jack to call me," he said forcefully. "Tomorrow, first thing. I don't care how early. He's got the number."

"Okay, I'll put the note on his desk myself."

"Thanks, Sue. I appreciate it."

"No problem. And Griffon—"

"Hmm?"

"I just wanted to let you know we think what you're doing is great. The secretaries took up a collection—almost three hundred dollars—and sent it off to that Neighborhood thing you're raising money for. And Dinah says Jack said they're going to put your picture on the cover of next month's program guide. The 'new you.' Isn't that something?"

Griff took a death grip on his temper. "It's something, all right. Look, Sue—"

"Oops! My other line's ringing. Gotta run. See you!"

"Just tell Sherwood—"

The line went dead.

"To *call* me," Griff finished in frustration and jammed the innocent receiver back into its cradle.

11

CAITI WASN'T QUITE SURE what she'd expected Denise's house to be like, but the white stucco building facing the verdant darkness of Golden Gate Park was a wonderful surprise. "What a great place for Peggy. It must be like having the whole park for a front yard!"

"Well, not quite," Griff said, maneuvering into a tight parking space. "Too much traffic for her to cross the street by herself yet. But it is beautiful." Turning off the ignition, he smiled at her. "Ready to face the Gorgon?"

Caiti felt her answering smile fade. "Griff, you promised you'd..." Then, with a surge of relief, she realized that he was teasing her. "You're a wicked, wicked man, Griff Falconer."

"Rotten to the core," he agreed. "And in desperate need of a kiss."

"Do you really think you deserve one, after that?" Caiti asked, unfastening her seat belt.

"Maybe not, but 'deserve' and 'need' are two separate issues. Besides, I guarantee I'll be on my best behavior for the rest of the night. You'll see. I'll be a paragon of virtue and restraint. A friendly, cheerful, smiling guest. On my honor, not a single angry word will pass these lips. And, speaking of lips..."

One kiss became two, then three, each a little longer, a little more enticing than the one before. Caiti broke from their fourth embrace in laughing confusion. "Wait, Griff. Wait! We're sitting here necking in a parked car like a couple of school kids."

"I know. Isn't it great?"

Caiti laughed again. "You want the truth? It's fantastic. But we've got a party to go to."

"We'll make our own party."

"Griff—"

"I know. I know." He slumped back against the seat. "Give me a minute. Damn, you get to me. For two cents I'd turn this car around and—"

"For three cents I'd help," Caiti agreed, trying to ignore the sweet ache in her loins. "But this is Nana's birthday party and we shouldn't be late. Besides," she said with a smile, "there's always *after* the party."

Griff brightened. "Yes, there is. There most certainly is! You can rest assured I'll keep that tempting thought in mind all evening while we're being charming and dutiful." He reached behind the seat and lifted a wine bottle and the gift-wrapped box containing Peggy's portraits from the floor of the car. "Well, shall we go in, Ms Kelly?"

"As you please, Mr. Falconer."

They crossed the sidewalk and mounted the porch steps in companionable silence. As Griff rang the doorbell, Caiti breathed a silent prayer for an uneventful evening.

The door swung open, revealing a slender man with thinning sandy hair and glasses. "Come in!" he said, stepping back out of their way. "You must be Griff and Caiti. I'm Sidney Fielding. Let me take your coats. Denise is in the kitchen but she'll be out in just a minute, and I think you'll find Peggy and our guest of honor in the dining room, roasting marshmallows."

"Doing what?" Caiti asked in amazement.

Sidney laughed. "Come on, I'll show you."

"You two go ahead," Griff urged. "I'll take this wine to the kitchen and greet our hostess."

Caiti gave him a last encouraging smile and let Sidney lead her off to the dining room where, true to his word, she found Nana and Peggy impaling miniature marshmallows on silver fish forks and browning them over a candle.

"Caitlin dear!" Nana greeted her. "Would you care for a marshmallow?"

Peggy put down her fork and ran to them. "Did you bring Nana's present? Where's Griffon? I helped make the salad, didn't I, Sidney?"

"Yes," Sidney agreed. "And I think your brother was carrying a box with a big white bow on it when he came. Why don't you run to the kitchen and see if that's the present?"

"Will you come, too?" Peggy asked, tugging his hand.

Sidney looked pleased, but he shrugged. "I'd like to, but I haven't heard the magic word yet."

"Please, Sidney? Please come with me?"

"All right. Would you rather walk or ride?"

"Ride, please!"

"If you'll excuse us," Sidney said to Caiti and Nana, and knelt down so that Peggy could climb on his back. "One of these days," he warned Peggy as he rose, groaning, "you're going to get too big for this game. Hang on!"

Caiti watched them go, then turned to smile at Nana. "Happy birthday. You make a very unconvincing eighty-four-year-old."

"Thank you, dear. It's sweet of you to say so, although there are days when I feel every year of it." She patted the chair beside her. "Here—push Arthur aside and sit down. You're looking lovely tonight. Have you been having a good time with Griffon?"

Interpreted one way it was a perfectly proper question. Interpreted the other . . . For the sake of her own peace of mind, Caiti decided the question had been asked innocently. "I've never met anyone quite like Griff," she replied. "And yes, I've been having a wonderful time."

"Good. I'm glad to hear you say so. Griffon's very dear to me. He's seemed happier these past few days than I've seen him in years, and I think I have you to thank for that." Nana's eyes twinkled. "Well, enough said. I just wanted you to know how pleased I am that the two of you have hit it off." She popped a tiny marshmallow into her mouth and chuckled. "I've heard it said that the urge to meddle is a sure sign of old age, so perhaps I'll have to admit to being eighty-four, after all."

A chorus of laughter carried to them dimly from the kitchen.

"Actually I'm beginning to think that Sidney may be as good for Denise as you are for Griffon," Nana observed.

"Has she known him long?"

Nana spread her hands. "Six months or so, I think, but I wouldn't swear to it. Denise and I aren't the closest of confidantes. I've heard her mention his name, but tonight is the first time I've actually met the man. Apparently he and his younger brother run a bookshop here in town. Perhaps—"

"Nana?" Peggy's voice was followed by the quick patter of her shoes along the hardwood floor of the hall. She appeared in the doorway, flushed with excitement, and announced importantly, "Mama says for everybody to come into the living room now so Nana can open up her presents and then we'll eat dinner and then we'll all have *cake!*"

"It sounds like an excellent plan," Nana said. "Are you going to help me up?"

Peggy ran to pull the old woman to her feet. "Hurry, Nana. Hurry!"

"Yes, dear, I will," Nana assured the little girl, and smiled at Caiti. "The world spins quickly when you're only four. Come along. We mustn't keep everyone waiting."

In the living room, Caiti settled herself to bask in the warmth of the fireplace as she watched Nana open her birthday presents: from Griff and Peggy, Peggy's portraits, now mounted and framed; from Denise, matinee tickets to a musical on tour from Broadway; and from Sidney, a leather-bound volume of Rudyard Kipling's poems. Feeling self-conscious, Caiti said, "I have a present for you, too, Nana, but I couldn't bring it tonight. It isn't quite ready yet."

"Dare I hope it will be a portrait of Griffon?"

Caiti nodded and smiled. "We've had one sitting already, but none of the pictures were quite what I had in mind for you. If you can talk Griff into sitting again, I'll promise to do better."

Nana's lips quirked in amusement. "Somehow I don't think you'll find another sitting too hard to arrange. Well, I certainly thank you all. Now, Peggy, perhaps Sidney would be kind enough to look on the mantel and see if there are any more presents there."

"I'd be glad to," Sidney said obligingly, turning to look. "Yes, I think you're right. There's one right here."

"And whose name is on the gift tag?" Nana asked.

Sidney examined it. "The card says 'For the third Marion, From the first Marion.' That doesn't tell me much. Who do you suppose I should give it to?"

"Me!" Peggy said, dancing with excitement. "It's for me! Nana's the first Marion, and Griffon's the second Marion, and I'm the third Marion, so it's for me, from Nana! Isn't it? Isn't that right?"

"Absolutely," Nana said. "It's my present to you, Peggy. Go ahead. Open it."

Wrapping paper flew, but Caiti's attention was divided. What was it Peggy had said? *Griffon's the second Marion.* What on earth had she meant by that?

"It's for wearing on very special occasions, like to-night," Nana was saying, and Caiti leaned forward with the others to admire the tiny locket on its thin gold chain. "And when it's time to go to bed tonight, you should give it to your mother so she can put it in her jewelry box and keep it safe for you. That locket belonged to my mother, and that makes it very old indeed. Do you like it?"

Peggy nodded, beaming.

"Well, then, let's ask your mother to fasten it for you. My fingers don't work too well on little chains these days."

"Thank you, Nana," Denise said, opening the tiny clasp. "It's beautiful. I'll see that she takes proper care of it. And now, if everyone's ready, we can eat." As they rose to their feet, she walked to Caiti's side. "I'm glad you could come tonight, Caiti. Is it still all right for me to pick up my copies of Peggy's pictures on Monday?"

"Anytime after noon," Caiti assured her. "Have you thought any more about modeling for me?"

Denise looked embarrassed but pleased. "I'd be will-ing, if you really want me to."

"Good! We can iron out the details on Monday."

Half a dozen times during the meal, Caiti found herself wishing for her camera. She wanted to capture the play of candlelight on Nana's Gibson Girl hairstyle, and the way Peggy kept tucking her chin to her chest in an attempt to look at her new locket. She wanted to capture Denise's bright animation as it became apparent that the party was a success. And, more than anything, Caiti wanted to cap-ture the endless play of emotion and expression on Griff's face, merry and sober, teasing and poignant by turns as he wove a web of table talk, including them all, uniting them all in an aura of celebration and good fellowship.

At Nana's request, there were only twelve candles on the cake. "The blue ones stand for decades," she explained, "and the white ones for years." She closed her eyes and made a wish and, with Peggy's help, blew the candles out.

When the last crumbs of cake had been consumed, Peggy looked across the table at Denise. "Now, Mama?" she asked.

Caiti was surprised to see a flush of color rise in Denise's cheeks. "All right. Now." Denise raised her voice slightly. "Everyone? Excuse me. Peggy has an announcement to make."

With a sense of theater that Caiti began to suspect ran in the family, Peggy waited until all eyes were focused on her, then burst out, "Sidney's going to come and live with us! He's going to be my new daddy!"

"We'll be getting married sometime next month," Denise clarified happily. "Just a small civil ceremony, but we hope you'll all be there."

"Congratulations," Caiti heard Griff say to Sidney with quiet sincerity, as Peggy sang a belated chorus of "Happy Birthday" and Nana admired Denise's engagement ring. "Let me know as soon as you set the date and I'll try to coax the extra vacation time out of FineArts."

Caiti's head came up with a snap. Across the table, Griff met her gaze for a startled instant, then looked away, as if the words had been as much a revelation to him as they were to her.

"Of course," Sidney agreed. "It's going to be sometime after the fifteenth, but Denise will let you know exactly."

Caiti felt the cheerful talk tumbling past her like water over stone, a meaningless babble.

He'll be going back to New York in a few days, she admitted to herself, and the thought was like a physical pain in her head, her heart. *He may go back for good, even if he wins the audition. And what will you do then?*

Sidney was moving around the table, filling the little cut-glass goblets at each place. "A toast," he said, and Caiti closed her numb fingers carefully around the slender stem. "To happily ever after."

Caiti forced a smile, determined not to ruin the evening for anyone else. "To happily ever after," she echoed with the others and sipped at the sweet dessert wine, bitter as aloe on her tongue.

DRIVING BACK to Nana's house, Griff found the trip a disconcertingly quiet one. Beside him, Nana nodded against her headrest, already half asleep after the excitement of the evening. Caiti was a wraith, huddled in the back seat. As the car passed from one street light to the next, the rearview mirror offered occasional glimpses of her, pale and silent, her face turned to the window. *Wait*, Griff counseled himself. *You can't solve anything with Nana sitting here, anyway. Just wait.*

When he finally brought the Volvo to a stop in front of Nana's house, he had to stifle a sigh of relief. Setting the parking brake, he walked around the car and opened the passenger door. "Nana? Rise and shine, birthday girl. You're home."

"I wasn't asleep," Nana asserted, then amended, "Well, perhaps I did doze, just for a moment." She unfastened her seat belt. "Good night, Caitlin. I'm so glad you could be at my party!"

"Good night, Nana," Caiti said brightly, "and happy birthday!" But Griff could hear the underlying tension in her tone.

Nana turned back to face him. "All right, Griffon. Do you think you can extricate me?"

"No problem. Just give me your hand. I'll be right back, Cait."

"Take your time," was all she said.

He helped Nana to her feet and guided her up the walkway to the front door. When she began to delve in her purse, searching for her elusive key ring, he ground his teeth impatiently. There was Caiti, sitting in the dark, thinking who knew what, and where was he? Cooling his heels on his grandmother's porch.

But even that thought brought a pang of guilt. How many more birthday celebrations would he and Nana be able to share?

"That was the nicest birthday party I've had in years," Nana said happily. "And the very nicest part was the way you and Denise got along."

"You have Caiti to thank for that," Griff admitted with a pang. "She made me take a good look at how Denise and I were acting and what it was doing to Peggy. I wasn't thrilled with what I saw. So I took Denise a bottle of wine tonight as a peace offering." He managed a crooked smile, remembering the look of confusion and suspicion on Denise's face when he'd presented the gift. "I'm still not claiming she's my favorite person in the world. But I think we made a start at a détente, tonight."

"It certainly looked that way to me, and it's bound to— Aha! My keys!" Nana unlocked the front door. "Well, you were a dear to drive me home."

"Yes, I'm the soul of generosity," Griff assured her wryly, stepping past her into the foyer to turn on the entryway light. "Especially when it's your car I'm driving!"

"Well, your duty's done now. I'm home, safe and sound, so set your mind at ease and get back to Caitlin. She's waited quite long enough to have you all to herself. And I promise not to worry if you're a little late tonight," she added with a knowing smile. "You two run along and enjoy yourselves."

Griff waited outside the door until he heard her slide the dead bolt home. Then, with a heavy heart, he walked back to the car.

Caiti had already moved from the back seat into the front. Sliding in behind the wheel, Griff said, "We need to talk."

"I know."

"Your place?" he asked, starting the engine. "Or don't you think that's a good idea? It's not all that late. We could find a restaurant, or a bar, if you'd rather talk...."

"In neutral territory?" She shook her head. "There's no need for that, Griff. We aren't going to argue. I'm just..." Again, she shook her head. "My apartment's fine."

Fifteen minutes later, Griff found himself in Caiti's living room again, studying the faces on the wall while she boiled a kettle of water. They had finished the drive in silence, but the time for silence was almost past.

She came into the room and set a tray on one of the end tables. "There's sugar or milk, but I don't have any lemon," she said, gesturing apologetically at the tray.

"No need. I don't put anything in my tea." Griff found himself wishing for a glimpse of Irish temper. There was something unsettling about her continued mildness. Lifting a mug from the tray, he sat down on the sofa. "Right now, I think 'no lemon' qualifies as the least of our worries."

Caiti claimed her own mug and sat at the far end of the couch, looking at him so intently that he fancied he could feel the movement of her gaze as it traveled over his face. "What do you want?" she asked.

Griff considered. The question was so open-ended that it seemed unanswerable. "I'm not sure what you mean, Cait."

"I mean a lot of things, I guess. I want—I need—to know what you want for yourself—from your job, from your life, from me." She frowned down at the steam rising from her mug. "Maybe what I need to know is whether you know what you want."

Griff hesitated. Somehow this wasn't how he had expected their talk to begin. "Does anybody?" he asked, trying not to sound defensive.

"Yes," Caiti replied.

"What about you?" he persisted, stung by her unqualified response. "Do *you* know what you want?"

"Yes. And I know what I'm doing about it."

"What, then?"

She slipped her shoes off and drew her feet up under her on the sofa cushion. "I want a chance to do what I do best—photography—so I work in the studio with Papa Tony. I want to feel good about myself and know I'm doing something for the people around me, so I volunteer my time to The Neighborhood." She blew on the surface of her tea and took a quick sip. "And I want to find out if you and I have any future together, so I'm sitting here, trying to talk to you about this, instead of just sending you home and crawling off to cry in the shower."

Crying in the shower. Was that how she had coped when her husband died? He wanted to ask, but he didn't feel he had the right. "Caiti, I—"

She watched him expectantly.

"I love you."

"You keep saying that," she said, shaking her head, "but it isn't enough. You have to decide what you're going to do about it. Besides what we did last night," she amended, with a tender wisp of a smile that spurred his pulse. The smile faded, leaving the curve of her lips soft and wistful. "Are you going back to New York, Griff?"

"I don't know."

"You seemed to know, when you were talking to Sidney."

"I said it without thinking. I've lived there quite a while now. It's where my job is."

"Is it a job you want to keep doing? If you could choose between working on 'Heroes & Heartbreakers' or being in Mr. Dunnett's theater troupe, which would you rather do?"

"It's not that simple," he objected.

"Why not? If Mr. Dunnett calls you on Friday and says they've picked you from the audition, what will you tell him, Griff? What do you want to tell him?"

"I don't know! All I know is that I love you, and I want to be with you. What if I do choose FineArts and go back to New York? Does that mean I lose you? Or would you come with me?"

"Come with you? Are you serious? Griff, if you choose FineArts, you'll be going back to New York in just a few days!"

"But you'd love it there," he insisted, as the idea caught fire in his mind. He gestured at the walls of portraits. "You like faces? New York has millions of them. You're good, Caiti. Really good. You could work up a portfolio and convince a gallery to exhibit your prints. Maybe even try a book!"

"And do what for food and rent, in the meantime?"

"Live with me," he said earnestly. "Be with me."

She looked troubled. "Live with you, be with you... but as what, Griff?"

"As yourself. As the woman I love."

"But not as your wife," she said quietly.

It was a fair question. He owed her an honest answer. "No. Not as my wife. It's not because I don't love you. I do. And I want to be with you. But marriage— Damn it, Cait, my father got married six times. Six times! On the rare occasions when marriage isn't a bribe or a weapon, it's a farce. When you have love, you don't need a lot of mumbo-jumbo to keep you together. And if the love fades, it's better to be able to end it without making some divorce lawyer richer."

"No," Caiti said, looking shaken. "Griff, marriages don't have to be like that. A marriage is what two people make it. To me, that means commitment. A foundation for building a life together. What I shared with Angelo wasn't a bribe *or* a weapon. And it certainly wasn't a farce. We were happy together, Griff. I loved him as much on the day he died as I did on our wedding day."

It was a threatening thought. "Maybe he was a better person than I am," Griff said heavily, and his dark thoughts elaborated, *or maybe you were just lucky Angelo died before the bubble could burst.* The mug in his hands seemed suddenly too heavy to hold. "Look, Caiti, I'm not saying there aren't any good marriages. I suppose there are some. But they're scarce, so scarce that it scares me." He lifted his shoulders in a small shrug. "Maybe things will look different to me, once we've lived together for a while—"

"I see," Caiti said sadly. "It's too soon for you to know whether you could take a chance on marrying me. But it's not too soon for me to leave my family, my job, my work with The Neighborhood and run away to New York with you? We need more time to think about all this."

"Apart?"

"If that's how it has to be. Griff, we've only known each other a week. Just a week."

"And you knew Angelo all your life. How can I compete with that? No matter how long you know me, it's always going to seem too soon, too hasty. Can't you just trust the love, Caiti? Can't you, for once in your life, just take a chance?"

She opened her eyes abruptly. "All right, Griff. I'll take a chance—if you will."

"What do you mean?" he asked uneasily.

"I'll come and live with you, here or in New York—your choice—if you'll shave off your beard."

Fear exploded within him. Desperately he twisted it into anger. "Damn it, Caiti, can't you think about anything but saving the fund-raiser? Is that what last night was about, too? Just another way to influence me? Another string you could pull?"

"No!" To his astonishment, there were tears in her eyes. "Forget the festival. Don't show up at all, if that's how you feel! That's not the point, not anymore. I thought Nana was crazy at first, but I see now that she was right. You're letting that beard and whatever it's hiding turn your whole life inside out. So you may have some scars. So what? So *what*? Do you think I'd love you one bit less?"

Griff stared at her in horror. "She told you about all that?"

Caiti put down her mug and surged to her feet, as if the couch were too small to hold the whirlwind of emotion that filled her. "Last night, you were so excited after your theater audition that you could hardly sit still, but you'll turn them down, you'll throw that chance away, you'll leave me here and go back to New York all alone rather than let anybody see your face without that beard, *won't* you?"

If Irish temper was what he had wanted to see, Caiti was obliging him now. "Cait—"

"Don't talk to *me* about trusting and being willing to take a chance, Griff Falconer. And don't kid yourself that I don't know what it might be like to be scarred and have to cope with people's reactions to that, day in and day out." She snatched the mug out of his hands and pulled him to his feet. "Look at that," she ordered, pointing to one of the larger photo portraits on the wall. "Do you know who that is?"

Griff found himself looking at the face of a young man with curly dark hair and laughing eyes. Only after he had noted those eyes and the air of exuberance the photograph had captured did his gaze stray to the young man's lopsided grin, and the line of scar tissue that broke the line of his upper lip and curved upward to the base of his nose.

"Well?" Caiti prodded.

With a terrible sense of despair, Griff said, "Angelo."

"And do you know what you're seeing?"

He nodded. "I've seen scars like that before, but not that bad. He must have been born with a hare lip."

"Yes. And you're right about the scars; there were complications with the corrective surgery. It wasn't the world's most aesthetic result, but it was functional. Angelo never wasted much worry on it." She crossed her arms, hugging her elbows as if the room were too cold. "Tell me the truth, Griff. Assuming you could keep your beard, which would you rather work for, FineArts or Mr. Dunnett's theater troupe?"

There was no escape except deceit, and he would not lie to her. "The theater troupe."

"And where would you rather live, here in San Francisco with Nana and Peggy, or in New York, alone?"

"Here."

"When Mr. Dunnett calls on Friday, if he offers you the position, are you going to turn it down?"

"Yes." It hurt to inhale.

"And your beard is the only reason?"

"Yes."

"Well then," she said soberly, the tears glinting again in her eyes, "we both have some thinking to do. Do you mind if I take a few days to decide?"

"To decide . . . ?"

"About your offer. To come and live with you in New York, no strings attached. I'll be thinking about it, Griff.

I really will. And I hope you'll be thinking about mine—we can be together and live wherever you like, if you'll shave off your beard." Her voice was steady, but she was trembling. "Let me know on Saturday, at the festival. And if we can't agree . . ." He glimpsed briefly what delivering the ultimatum was costing her, and wondered if he would have the strength to walk away. The light clarity of her voice was a counterpoint to the dull pulse pounding in his ears and the sharp grief rising in his heart. It all sounded so logical: here's what I want, here's what you want, now we have to choose. But of the two of them, only he knew that the deck was stacked and that nobody could win.

Caiti came to him slowly and leaned her forehead against his chest. "Griff, please, think all this through. Don't do yourself out of what you want the most when there may not even be a reason." Raising her head, she took his hand. "I know you may still find some scarring if you shave away your beard. But maybe you won't. And then there wouldn't be any problem at all! At least it's a fifty-fifty chance."

He couldn't lie to her—not even by his silence. Dropping her hand, he stepped away. "No. It's no chance at all."

"What do you mean?"

"I know exactly what I'd find under the beard." Griff picked up his jacket and walked slowly to the door. "That's why I won't shave it off."

Caiti still stood across the room, where he'd left her, as if she lacked the strength to take one more step. "You know? How could you know?"

There was one final truth to tell. "Because," he said, taking a last long look at her before he walked out. "There aren't any scars. There never were."

12

THE ALARM RANG at seven. Silencing it with uncharacteristic force, Caiti burrowed deeper beneath the covers, unwilling to face the new day.

"There are no scars. There never were." All night, Griff's bewildering confession had echoed through her mind, troubling her dreams. She was heartsick over the hard words they'd exchanged, but despite the pain, it seemed to Caiti that it had all been inescapable, a thicket of thorny growth that had to be excised before she and Griff could hope to reach each other and be free.

She'd meant every word she said. She had no wish to take back a single phrase. And yet she did regret that, out of all the words they'd thrown at each other, she still had not offered him the ones he had told her so freely: I love you.

Was it fair to expect him to accept or reject her proposal when she hadn't told him, in those dangerously simple words, what he had come to mean to her?.She could call him and tell him now—but after last night, would he even want to hear?

As if triggered by her thoughts, the telephone rang.

It could be Griff. It could be. She snatched the receiver from its cradle and retreated with it beneath the warm covers. "Hello?"

"Caitlin? It's Nana. Are you all right?"

"I'm fine," Caiti assured her, worried by the agitation in Nana's voice. "Is something wrong?"

"I don't know. I don't understand what's happening." Nana sounded close to tears. "Did you and Griffon have a fight last night? I don't know why he'd go. I don't know what to do about it."

"Nana, what's happened? Are you saying Griff is gone?"

"That's what I'm trying to tell you! I just woke up and found a note from him on my bedside table."

Caiti fought against a rising sense of panic. One part of her mind was floundering against Nana's words in disbelief and confusion. But another calmer part already seemed to know. "Where is he?" she asked, determined to hear the words. "What does the note say?"

Nana sighed. "It says he's gone back to New York."

RECLINING HIS SEAT, Griff put on the headphones and closed his eyes to discourage the attentions of the cheerful flight attendants. He should have remembered that flying first class meant less privacy than coach, not more. But the coach seats had all been sold, and he'd felt compelled to be on his way, not wanting to wait even an hour for the next flight.

He'd been up all night thinking—or trying to—when Jack Sherwood's call came through shortly after six, as he'd suspected it would. "You said you didn't care how early I called" had been Jack's first defensive words, and his exiting speech ten minutes later had been even more pugnacious. "Don't tell *me* you aren't going to do it. We're *way* past that point, bucko. You'll do it, all right, or I'll have your ears for ashtrays and that beard of yours for a necktie. Hell, if you try to back out now, I'll have your job! You can't *do* this to me!"

And so Griff was flying to New York to face them down, uncomfortably aware of the unsigned contract. Jack Sherwood might have just enough clout to make good on his threat. A fine mess that would leave him in: no "Heroes & Heartbreakers," no Golden Gate Players, no Caiti....

Forget the job. He could find another job if he had to. But Caiti was another matter altogether.

"There are no scars," he'd told her stubbornly, but he knew that it was only half true. Beneath the beard his face was untouched, but the past had left an indelible mark on him, all the same. People like Angelo Buonarroti could turn to plastic surgeons, but what hope was there when the scars were deep inside, invisible to everyone but him?

Caiti had probably heard from Nana by now. Did she hate him or just pity him for running off to New York to cover his bets?

He should have tried to explain it all to her, but how could anyone else understand the web of frustration and anger, guilt and self-loathing that had enveloped him after the accident? With his right wrist in a cast, shaving had been an awkward aggravation that he had soon foregone. Within weeks his features were obscured by a rough stubble of beard . . . and the people on campus began to treat him in a whole new way, a way that was based on what he said and did, not how he looked.

It had seemed like a perfect solution, just as it had seemed kinder to mislead Nana about the extent of his injuries than to explain to her that the name and bone structure he had inherited from her were making his life a living hell.

But now his clever solution had caught up with him, and what had originally been a personal and reasonable decision now seemed dishonest and unkind. To deserve Caiti, a man would have to be a hero—not some radio big mouth afraid to face his own reflection, but a real hero: a man who was quietly confident of his strengths, did honest battle with his weaknesses and knew where he was going with his life.

Griff felt bone weary, far beyond what one night of lost sleep could account for. He switched his headphones to the classical channel, hoping the music would lull him. There'd be plenty of time later to think about what losing Caiti would do to him. Plenty of time.

Maybe a lifetime.

"I NEED the morning off," Caiti said.

Antonio Buonarroti looked up from the morning newspaper, his face a picture of astonishment.

"I'll try to be back by lunchtime," she promised, buttoning her jacket while she talked. "I know I said I'd do the rest of the developing this morning, but it's going to have to wait."

"You have had a call from The Neighborhood?" Papa Tony suggested. "An emergency, perhaps?"

"An emergency, yes, but not with The Neighborhood."

The surprise left his face, supplanted by a sympathetic smile. "Something to do with your young man, then. Whatever has happened, I see that you are going to go out and do battle for him. I hope he is worthy."

"He is, Papa." She kissed his forehead. "He is. He just doesn't know it yet."

STANDING ON THE STEPS of the old Victorian, using the brass door knocker, Caiti had experienced a bittersweet flash of déjà vu. If she closed her eyes and wished for it hard enough, would a voice from the fog ask, "Looking for me?"

Now, settled in the study with Nana, the sense of Griff's presence was even stronger. Drawing strength from it, Caiti put down her teacup. "What did Peggy mean, last night, when she said Griff was the 'second Marion'?"

Nana looked surprised. "Just that he was named after me—Marion Griffon Falconer. Silly and sentimental, I know, but my daughter Amelia insisted. I told her it would be quite enough just to give him my maiden name, Griffon, but she was determined, and I didn't see any point in disputing it with her. After all, she meant it as a compliment, and Marion *has* been a man's name for centuries." She dimpled. "Even John Wayne's first name was Marion, you know. Anyway, no one's called Griff that in years."

It was another piece of the puzzle, whether Caiti could understand its significance yet or not. "But they used to?"

"Oh, yes. Until he went off to college, really. And then, when Peggy was born, Colin was adamant that *she* be named Marion, as well. I think he had some peculiar notion that I'd love Peggy more if she were named after me. That I'd think of her as being my grandchild, just as Griffon was. Technically, of course, she isn't any relation to me at all, and I think he was afraid she wouldn't benefit from my estate. Silly, grasping man. I love Peggy for her own sweet sake, and my 'estate' hardly warrants so grand a word."

"Yes," Caiti said, keeping her voice carefully casual, "Griff was saying that most of what you have is tied up in renovating the house."

Nana made a reluctant sound of assent and sipped her tea.

Caiti looked at her with fond exasperation. "Then don't you think you'd better forget all that lofty talk about 'resources' and bailing out The Neighborhood?"

Nana looked startled, then affronted. "Oh, but I meant every word of what I said!" she protested. "If I mortgage the house, I could repay The Neighborhood for the donations it will lose and—"

"And do what, then, to meet the payments?" Leaning forward, she took one of Nana's fragile hands in her own. "No. Even if Griff stays in New York and the fund-raiser goes belly-up, I wouldn't want you to do that—for his sake as much as for yours. Can you imagine how it would make him feel, when he found out?"

"I wouldn't tell him," Nana said with stiff-lipped pride.

"I would," Caiti retorted just as firmly, and watched as the starch went out of Nana's shoulders. "You owe it to Griff and Peggy to keep this house in the family, unencumbered, if you possibly can. And you owe it to yourself. Do you think Griff would ever have felt free to try his wings in New York if he hadn't known you had a roof safely over your head?"

"But it's entirely my fault that The Neighborhood stands to lose the money."

"Not entirely. You may have started the ball rolling, but FineArts gave it a pretty hefty push, too. And even if worse comes to worst, it isn't like The Neighborhood's going to be forty thousand dollars in debt; we just won't have that extra income to rely on." She grimaced. "Sure, we'd rather have the money than not have it. But we can get along without it, if we have to."

"I still feel—"

"Nana, be sensible. Someday you may be faced with an emergency and really *need* to mortgage the house. But this isn't it. I can't stop you from doing it, but I'll bet I can talk The Neighborhood out of accepting the proceeds. It would feel like blood money, and I couldn't face that. Besides," she said, determined to lighten the heavy conversation, "rumor has it that the plumbing still needs work."

"You've been listening to Griffon," Nana accused with a grudging smile.

"Trying to," Caiti agreed. "But it isn't always easy. Our shared vocabulary doesn't reach into all the dark corners. I was hoping you could shed a little light for me."

"What do you mean?"

"Could you tell me more about Griff?"

"You mean what he was like, those summers he spent with me, when he was a little boy? Well, of course, dear, if that's what you want. And I can show you the family photograph album. But isn't it all rather like locking the barn door after the horse has been stolen?"

Caiti shook her head stubbornly. "I won't believe that. It's not too late. Not yet. Griff may change his mind."

"And if he doesn't?"

Caiti sighed. "We've got until noon on Saturday, and I intend to use every minute."

"To do what, Caitlin?"

"To figure out that grandson of yours. And I'm going to, even if I have to become a blend of Sherlock Holmes and Sigmund Freud to do it."

"Well, in that case," Nana said, lifting down a leather-bound album from one of the massive bookshelves, "you'd better have a look at this. And I can give you all of the letters Griffon sent me each year while he was away at boarding school."

Caiti's throat tightened. "Oh, Nana, are you sure? Those must be very special to you, very private...."

"Of course I'm sure," Nana said decisively and smiled. "Judging by the look in your eye, I suspect it's time I got used to sharing him with you."

WHEN GRIFF OPENED his apartment door and stepped inside, he felt as if he'd been away for years, not weeks.

According to the hasty schedule he'd made before he left San Francisco, he had expected to go straight to the FineArts offices and nail Jack Sherwood to the wall. But a forty-minute layover in Denver had stretched into hours as they waited for weather conditions to stabilize. By the time he deplaned in New York, it was almost too late to call FineArts from the airport and lodge his demand for a meeting the following morning.

But now, after a day of travel and delays and frustrations, he was home.

Home. The word had never sounded so empty to him.

He turned on a lamp, but the small oasis of light only made the apartment look more forlorn than before. Standing in the doorway, he found himself wondering if it had always looked so barren. He wished he'd been less organized about arranging for his absence. Instead of a distracting clutter of junk mail and moldy meat loaf, he was faced with an empty mailbox, an empty refrigerator... an empty life.

Annoyed by the tide of self-pity he could sense rising inside, he strode into the bedroom and picked up the telephone. At least he could call Nana and apologize for his predawn departure....

But nothing, it seemed, was going to go right. When Nana's telephone had rung twenty times, he finally hung up. Feeling challenged, he dialed Denise's number—and again listened as a distant phone rang and rang and rang, unanswered.

Damn it, he wasn't going to be stopped so easily. All he wanted was to fall into bed and sleep, but he wasn't going to face a guilty conscience in the morning. If Nana and Denise weren't answering, he'd call Caiti!

No, he realized a moment later, he wouldn't. Or, more accurately, couldn't. In their giddy week together, he'd never bothered to write down her phone number, even after learning it was unlisted.

For a moment he stood motionless, feeling totally balked. Then his tired mind unearthed an alternative. A call to the information operator yielded one last number. Feeling grimly self-satisfied, Griff dialed it.

But when his call was answered on the fifth ring, and he heard Papa Tony's bass voice announce, "Buonarroti Studios," his own voice caught in his throat.

"Hello?" the disembodied voice said. "Hello?"

There was nothing he could say, no explanation he could make, no message he could leave. There were only decisions to be made and actions to be taken. With a crushing sense of futility, Griff lowered the receiver back into its cradle.

THROUGH THE LONG afternoon of work in the studio and darkroom, Caiti resisted the temptation to carry Nana's album with her. She was anxious to explore the letters and photographs it held, but they deserved her full attention, and so did her work. After five o'clock, her time would be her own—or so she thought until the phone call from The Neighborhood came. "Caiti? There's been a kitchen fire at Henderson's Café. A bunch of us are going over to help Sam clean up. It's a real mess. Can we count on you?"

When she walked into Henderson's Café twenty minutes later, it was obvious that water from the sprinkler system had done nearly as much harm as the fire itself. Soot-stained rivers marred the floor and soaked slowly into stacks of tablecloths and napkins, as the wallpaper began to peel. Armed with mops and pails, Caiti and the others worked against time, trying to minimize the damage and salvage what they could.

Throughout most of the night a corner of her mind stayed focused obstinately on Griff, asking the same fruitless questions, replaying their last confrontation again and again, as if reviewing it could change the outcome. As the hours dragged past, the determination she'd displayed to Nana and to Papa Tony began to seem like nothing more than wishful thinking, and she sank, at last, into a purely mechanical effort that sustained her until the crew finally called a halt.

It was three in the morning when she reached home, reeking of smoke and reeling with fatigue. In a daze she stripped off her clothes and dropped them into a plastic garbage bag, sealing it to isolate the sickening smell of fire and destruction. It was willpower alone that kept her awake through a shower to wash away the filth and the stench, and desperation that prompted her to offer a brief prayer for herself and Griff—for a peaceful night, for hope, for a clear head. Then, exhausted, she crawled beneath the covers and tumbled headlong into sleep.

"WHETHER I'M PLANNING to go through with it or not isn't the point," Griff insisted doggedly. "The point is that I knew nothing about this charade until long after you started promoting it. I never promised anybody anything, and Jack knew that perfectly well when he sold you on the idea."

The assorted board members and senior staff offered no response. It was only eight-thirty, and most of them appeared to be more interested in their morning coffee than in his impassioned claim of unfair tactics.

"All right," Griff said, lowering his voice to a more reasonable level, "maybe this doesn't have to be so black and white. I've already agreed to a possible compromise with—" Caiti's face took shape in his memory, so familiar, so dear... Shaken, he blinked it away. "With the young woman who's coordinating the festival. I've told her I'd be willing to do a public reading and let them trim my hair and beard—"

"No." The flat rejection came from Harvey Gettleman, executive producer of "Heroes & Heartbreakers." "Our attorneys would have a fit. We've made some very specific claims in our promotional ads. The beard's got to go."

Griff tried a change of tactics. "Has my past work been satisfactory?"

"Of course it has," said Thelma Rivers, the FineArts program coordinator. "You know it has been."

"And was my salary demand for next season unreasonable?"

"No. But—" She looked past Jack Sherwood to Tim Flannigan, the Director of "Heroes & Heartbreakers." "Can't you make him see reason, Tim? Regardless of what he's telling us, the network has spent a lot of time and money promoting his appearance at this Neighborhood festival. If he backs out now—"

"I haven't said I won't do the fund-raiser," Griff interrupted.

"Then what are we arguing about?" Tim asked testily. "If you're going through with it, let's sign the damn contract and get on with the day. I don't know about the rest of you, but I've got a week's worth of work to do by noon."

"Hold on, Tim. I haven't said I *will* do it, either." A disgruntled murmur ran through the group. Griffon surveyed the half circle of faces, measuring their reactions. "When Jack returned my call yesterday, he threatened to get me fired if I didn't follow through on this fund-raiser. So I dropped everything and flew in here and asked for this meeting to find out whether that was the real situation or just so much hot air. And that's what I need to know from all of you, now. If I decide not to do this fund-raiser, do I still have my job?"

They balked; they hemmed and hawed; they conferred.

Griff waited in stony silence.

Finally it was Thelma Rivers who said, "This is a complicated situation, Griffon. I agree with you that Jack shouldn't have gotten FineArts involved if he didn't have your guarantee that you'd cooperate. But it was your own grandmother who contacted us. I'd say we acted in good faith. And we're publicly committed. So we're asking you to be a good team player. You'll do that for us, won't you?"

"I may. But I want a simple yes or no, Thelma. If I refuse to take part in the festival, will the new contract offer be rescinded?"

"If you refuse?" She looked at him unhappily. "Yes."

"And if I offer to take part according to the compromise I worked out with the festival committee? Would that be considered a refusal, too, as far as FineArts is concerned?"

She flicked a quick glance at Harvey Gettleman. "I'm afraid so."

"All right. At least we understand each other, now." He took the envelope out of his pocket and held it out to her. "My resignation."

"But—" Tim Flannigan gaped. "Damn it, Griff, you said you hadn't decided about the fund-raiser yet!"

"I haven't. But there's one thing I *have* decided. I'm not interested in working here anymore." He dropped the envelope onto the desk.

They stared at it, and then at him, their faces caricatures that could have been labeled Amazement, Outrage, Stunned Dismay. Before the tirade could begin, Griff turned his back and walked out of the office, out of the building, out into the crisp morning air.

IT WAS NEARLY eleven o'clock before Caiti opened her eyes on Friday morning. Blinking at the sunshine that poured across her bed, she reached for the telephone and dialed the studio's number.

"Good morning," a familiar voice chirped. "Buonarroti Studios."

"Mrs. Ames!" Caiti found that seven hours of sleep had revived her ability to laugh. "Have I slept straight through to Saturday?"

"Good morning, dear. Of course not. Didn't Antonio tell you? I traded Saturday for Friday this week so I wouldn't have to miss the festival tomorrow."

Tomorrow. Caiti felt suddenly queasy. "Has anybody called for me this morning?"

"Just Mrs. Billinger," came the answer, and Caiti's hopes rose. "She said she was going out to have lunch with a friend of hers but she'd call you again later."

Probably Daniel Dunnett, Caiti reflected, wanting to tell Nana about the audition committee's decision. "Thanks for taking the message, Mrs. Ames. Tell Papa I'll be out to help in a few minutes."

"No, he said you should have a nice lazy day for a change. Fix yourself something to eat and relax."

"But I already took yesterday morning off," Caiti protested.

"And the world didn't end, did it? Believe me, dearie, everything's in hand. You just suit yourself today."

Caiti's thoughts strayed to the photo album, still on the end table in the living room where she had dropped it yesterday, its cover unopened, its mysteries unexplored. "Okay, Mrs. Ames. Maybe I'll take you up on that offer, after all."

RETURNING to his apartment, Griff headed straight for the telephone. When Nana's number still went unanswered, he swore softly. Where the devil was she? It was a quarter to twelve in San Francisco. She must have met a friend for lunch. Why couldn't she stay home and knit by the fire, like other people's grandmothers?

The image was incongruous enough to make him smile. She'd never be Whistler's Mother—he wouldn't have wanted her to be—but there were times when her busy schedule, combined with her "early to bed, early to rise" philosophy, made her a hard woman to contact.

Griff looked at his watch and sighed. He'd just have to try her again from the airport.

MORNING EVAPORATED into afternoon as Caiti read Griff's letters. The earliest of them were laboriously printed on lined paper; the last few were typed; but the bulk of them were written in a flowing hand that Caiti had no trouble reconciling with her image of Griff. They were long and colorful and literate, detailing his adventures and misadventures with a candor that alternately chilled and wrung Caiti's heart.

As if she were reading an epistolary novel, Caiti began to recognize recurring characters. No labels of good or bad were applied, but Caiti could soon categorize them for herself. Letters that mentioned Tonker or Mr. Nevins were usually cheerful; letters containing the names Eddie or Kevin or Bill invariably ended on a more wistful note, sometimes with undisguised admissions of homesickness and pleas for deliverance.

The photographs in Nana's family album were a further revelation. Page after page was filled with photographs of Griff, as an angel-faced baby, a seraphic toddler, a beautiful young boy; in each picture he stood beside a lovely young woman, rarely the same one twice. And then, as the boy began to mature into a young man, the pictures stopped.

Nana's phone call, when it came, dragged Caiti out of her historical research and into the present with a vengeance. "I can't find him. I can't find him anywhere!"

"Nana, calm down. Where are you?"

"I'm at Daniel's. They want Griffon, Caitlin. The audition committee has selected him. There was no answer at his apartment, so I left a message on his answering machine and called the FineArts offices, but they said he didn't work there anymore!"

"What?" Caiti put down the letter she'd been reading. "Are you sure? Who did you talk to?"

"That Mr. Sherwood. He claims that Griffon resigned this morning—that they insisted he take part in the festival as planned, and he quit and walked out and they haven't seen him since. He says they may sue, Caitlin. He says—"

"People say a lot of things when they're angry," Caiti assured her, trying to sound sensible. "They can't do anything yet. Not until we see what happens at the festival."

"You don't honestly think Griffon will be here for it, do you? Not now. Not after this."

"I don't know," she said, astounded that none of her inner panic was audible. "Nobody knows now, except Griff. We'll just have to wait and see. But I don't think you should give up on him yet, Nana. I haven't. Tell Mr. Dunnett that he and the committee will have to wait until tomorrow for Griff's answer."

"But, Caitlin—"

"Nana, you believed in him all those years when nobody else did, when nobody else even cared. Don't stop now. Please. Just give him one more day."

BY MIDNIGHT Caiti's mind was filled with Griff's words, Griff's thoughts, Griff's face as it had been at five years old, and ten, and fifteen. With his old letters and photographs spread on the bed around her, Caiti sent her thoughts back over the familiar treadmill one final time and found, to her surprise, that while the facts remained the same, her conclusions had begun to alter.

"Come to New York with me," he had invited. But for all her fine words to the contrary, in her heart of hearts she had dismissed his suggestion as unfair and undesirable. How could he ask her to give up everything to go with him—her family, her friends, her job, her work with The

Neighborhood—when he wouldn't even promise her forever? She had asked that question in her mind again and again, angrily, accusingly, turning it into an answer.

But suppose she accepted Griff's plan for a year or so, long enough to explore their true feelings for each other. What would she actually be risking?

Family? Did she really believe that Papa Tony would love her any less if she moved away for a year? He might think she was making a mistake, but he would probably encourage her even then, if her alternative was a return to the cloistered existence she had lead before Griff exploded into her life.

Friends? It wouldn't really concern any of them, except Nana. And Nana would hardly object, not if it was what she and Griff wanted.

Her job? Nonsense. Her photography could be done anywhere, and Papa Tony would almost certainly take her back to work at the Buonarroti Studios again if she asked him to.

Her work with The Neighborhood? She would miss it, if Griff chose for them to live somewhere other than San Francisco, but there was no longer a serious shortage of volunteers. As much as it might pain her to admit it, The Neighborhood would run just as smoothly without her.

What other objection was left? She wasn't hypocritical enough to pretend to herself that it was a purely moral question. She was a grown woman, a widow, well aware of the give and take of love. It was true that she'd kept to herself since Angelo's death, avoiding any casual entanglements, but this was different. She had shared her body willingly with Griff, and she hoped with all her heart that their first night together wouldn't prove to be their last.

So then, what did she stand to lose if she agreed to Griff's plan and their life together didn't work out?

Her heart.

But wasn't it already Griff's to cherish or break as he saw fit? Was she prepared to lose him now, on principle alone? Or would she find the courage to throw her heart over the moon in a wild gamble for love and trust Griff to catch it as it fell and, in time, learn to keep it safe from harm?

She was operating from a foundation of strength and security. Griff was contemplating a leap from one cliff edge to another, with a long, dark drop between. If one of them had to be the first to trust, the first to dare, wouldn't it be fairer to take the burden on herself?

When Griff said he loved her and wanted to be with her, she believed him. She believed *in* him. But she was only beginning to discover the lifetime of fears and insecurities he would have to resolve before he could come to her unafraid. If she gave him the gift of a year, it might provide a climate where those fears could fall away naturally. In time he would be able to see that nothing was holding him back but himself. And then they could both come home. Together.

It was a risk, but it was a risk she could live with. She would follow her heart—if he ever came back to hear her decision.

"He'll be there tomorrow," she said out loud to the silent room as she gathered his letters and pictures and set them safely aside. "He'll be there," she said again and climbed into bed and turned off the light. "He will," she whispered to the darkness. "He just has to be."

FESTIVAL SATURDAY had dawned, but barely. During the night, fog had settled over the city, engulfing the upper reaches of buildings and hills, but the outer atmosphere was powerless to dampen the glow of the festival. In just a few short hours, the classrooms of the St. Swithin Academy had been transformed into booths and boutiques, and the gymnasium was filled to overflowing with eager patrons, each cheerfully paying a quarter a dance as the band swung its way from "The Beer Barrel Polka" to "The Tennessee Waltz," and on to a rowdy rendition of the "Virginia Reel."

Caiti had helped to oversee it all, hurrying up one hall and down another, answering questions, praising harried helpers and taking photographs. It had been a hard morning, but the hardest part of all had been accepting the compliments and congratulations of her fellow volunteers. They were predicting a triumph, and only Caiti and Nana knew that it might yet be a disaster.

At eleven-thirty the auditorium doors opened. By eleven forty-five every seat was filled. By five minutes to the hour video crews were crouched in the aisles, and the crowd was buzzing with anticipation. Griff was scheduled to appear on stage at noon.

He'll be here, Caiti had promised herself, but the auditorium was packed to capacity and Jacques D'Arnot of Shear Elegance had long since passed from nervousness into near-hysterical impatience.

"And where is he?" the temperamental stylist demanded from his vantage point in the wings. "Because you ask, I donate my time, my skills, Miss Kelly. All I ask of Mr. Falconer is that he present himself. Is that beyond him? Faithful clients go unsatisfied so that *I* can be here, at the time you requested. Am I an apprentice, a one-chair *barber*, to be kept waiting like this?" Still complaining, he stalked off to stand with his assistants.

Caiti scanned the crowded auditorium, praying for a glimpse of rust and auburn, auburn and rust. In the front row sat Papa Tony and Mrs. Ames. On their left were Denise and Sidney, Nana and Peggy. On Peggy's lap, Arthur was wearing a blue ribbon in honor of the day.

Meeting Nana's eyes, Caiti gave her head the smallest of shakes: no Griff.

Heartsick, she forced herself to face facts. It was noon—time to explain to the audience that Griffon Falconer wasn't coming, after all. Time to face the inevitable anger and loss of reputation, the demands for money back. And time to lay her personal dreams to rest, as well. There would be no second chance to build a life with Griff, in New York or anywhere else. The failure of this day would always stand between them as a reproach, an insurmountable barrier.

Wanting to cry, to mourn, Caiti walked to center stage. As soon as she stepped beyond the curtain, a thunder of applause rose from the audience. Embarrassed, she gestured, asking for silence.

"Hello," she said as soon as she thought she could make herself heard.

The microphone squealed with feedback.

Schooling her nerves, Caiti waited while adjustments were made.

"Hello," she said again, and this time her amplified voice floated out over the sea of expectant faces assembled there. "On behalf of The Neighborhood, I'd like to thank all of you for coming today. We're only as useful as you'll let us be, and we do appreciate your support." She licked her dry lips. "As some of you may know, this is our third annual festival."

She waited for the polite smattering of applause to die down.

"Each year we try to make our festival a little bigger, a little better, so that we can raise a little more money to support our work in the community. Well, this year we decided to try to turn that 'little' into a lot. We sent out flyers about Griffon Falconer—"

Again, the applause flared.

"And you responded," Caiti said. "In fact, you overwhelmed us with your response. We never expected so many of you to want to be involved. It was wonderful. But it makes it just that much harder for me to stand up here in front of you all, now, and so—"

"And so I think I'll join you," said The Voice from behind the crowd, clearly audible without a mike.

The audience cheered.

To Griff, nothing seemed real but the sight of Caiti, spotlit on the stage. The applause around him was white noise, the carpeted aisle just one more road to travel on his long journey back to her. In the past twenty-four hours he had ridden in airplanes, trains and taxicabs, delayed by blizzards and fog. Through it all, one phrase had echoed in his mind, like a mantra: *Coming home to Caiti, coming home to Caiti, coming home . . .*

Watching as he walked down the aisle toward her, Caiti thought her heart would burst, not just with relief—though her relief was profound—but with the pure unalloyed joy of seeing him. She wanted to throw herself into his arms and make him promise never, never to leave her alone again, but she couldn't move, could hardly stand as the happiness weakened her knees and clogged her throat.

Reaching the edge of the stage, Griff bounded up the final steps and came to put his arms around her. When the audience shouted their approval, he stole a kiss, then drew her skillfully back, away from the microphone.

"Sorry you had to wait," he panted, grinning. "I did hurry."

Recognizing the words he had first spoken to her on Nana's front porch, Caiti's eyes filled with tears. Smiling through the blur, she said quickly, "Daniel Dunnett called. They want you, Griff. They want you. I knew they would!"

Griff gave her shoulders a gentle squeeze. "Better save the details for later. Right now it's time you found a seat, camera lady. The show's about to begin."

Somehow she made her way down the steps and, at Nana's insistence, sat down in Peggy's seat, while Sidney took Peggy and Arthur onto his lap. On stage, while Griff spoke quietly to M. D'Arnot, the stylist's assistants brought out the equipment: a portable sink borrowed from the school's chemistry lab, a large apronlike covering, a little rolling table of combs and scissors and razors, and the chair itself.

"I'll let your tame barber cut my hair and trim my beard," Griff had promised, and he was here, now, sitting down in the chair, letting them arrange the drape, preparing to keep his word.

The haircut came first, and Caiti was relieved to see that M. D'Arnot's reputation was well-founded. Snipping away at the wayward nimbus of Griffon's hair, he retained its sense of free-spirited dash, fashioning a cut that was controlled without being conservative.

Then, lifting a different pair of scissors from the tray, he cut away a huge handful of Griff's beard.

Horrified, Caiti leaped to her feet, but Nana jerked her down again. "Sit still," she admonished, a fierce smile of pride on her face. "The boy knows what he's doing."

Tuft by tuft, the protective whiskers were trimmed off and swept carefully away, leaving a ragged auburn stubble, which, in turn, vanished beneath a cloud of shaving lather.

As M. D'Arnot's razor began its work, Caiti found herself holding her breath. All her well-intentioned amateur psychology could well be wrong, and Griff might end up hating her for forcing him out from behind his beard. He'd spent his entire childhood in the shadow of his father's

preoccupation with physical beauty; he'd watched as
stepmother after stepmother was married as an ornament
and later discarded as damaged goods; at boarding school,
he'd endured the teasing that his own good looks and un-
usual name had elicited. And, in the end, he had opted out,
refusing to expose himself to a world that judged on ap-
pearances.

But he had grown and matured in the intervening years.
She hoped—she believed—that he would come to realize
that his beard was a defense that had outgrown its use-
fulness, doing him far more harm than good.

Nana's hand tightened suddenly around hers, as M.
D'Arnot turned to the microphone and said pompously,
"Ladies and gentlemen, allow me to present Griffon Fal-
coner."

Rising from the chair, Griff stepped up to take the microphone, without even a mustache to hide behind. Revealed, his face was the one she had seen in Nana's
album—fine-boned, with the pure delicacy of a Botticelli
angel . . . but with a subtle difference. There was beauty,
yes, but the hollows beneath the high cheekbones and the
character lines around the sensitive mouth made it a
beauty tempered now by the pain of self-knowledge and
maturity.

The applause began again. As Griff waited for it to ebb,
his eyes sought Caiti's, and his smile wavered uncertainly.

Beaming up at him, she mouthed, "I love you!"

His answering smile, as he launched into the promised
reading, was blindingly luminous.

When the reading was over, he raised his hand to quiet
the crowd's applause. "Thank you, all of you," he said,
sending that shining smile out over the crowd. "If you'll

bear with me just a minute longer, I'd like to make a short announcement."

A receptive hush fell over the crowd.

"Some of you may have listened to me on 'Heroes & Heartbreakers' from time to time," he said diffidently, and waited while the crowd's laughter rose and fell. "Well, I'd like you all to be among the first to know that the season of programs that's currently airing will be my last on the show." He waved their protesting howls aside and continued, "Instead, if I can believe a message I've been given—"

Caiti nodded emphatically.

"—I'll be signing on as a new member of the Golden Gate Players, right here in San Francisco. So now, if you'll excuse me, I'm going to go sign my contract with the Players, before they have a chance to come to their senses." He let them laugh, and added, "But before I go, there's one item of business left to attend to. If Ms Kelly would be kind enough to join me again . . . ?"

Kind enough? There was nothing she wanted more. Caiti climbed the steps and hurried to his side.

"I think we'd all like a chance to publicly thank Caitlin Kelly, the woman who made this festival possible," Griff said loudly into the microphone. Then, under cover of the clamor of applause he'd incited, he murmured, "Sweet Cait, please, will you marry me?"

For a moment, in the tumult, she doubted her ears. But there was no doubting the look in his eyes. "Yes," she assured him. "Yes!"

"I'll understand if you need time to think it over. You're all I've ever wanted, all I'll ever need, but that doesn't mean that marrying me is the right decision for you to—"

Reaching up, Caiti stroked his naked jaw line. "'How like a man!'" she quoted, knowing he would recognize the lines from *Cyrano de Bergerac*. "'You think a man who has a handsome face must be a fool.'"

And she kissed him, with all the joy in her heart, while the audience went wild.

Harlequin American Romance®

Gull Cottage

The sun, the surf, the sand...

One relaxing month by the sea was all Zoe,
Diana and Gracie ever expected from their
four-week stay at Gull Cottage, the luxurious
East Hampton mansion. They never thought
that what they found at the beach would
change their lives forever.

Join Zoe, Diana and Gracie for the summer of
their lives. Don't miss the GULL COTTAGE
trilogy in Harlequin American Romance: #301
CHARMED CIRCLE by Robin Francis (July
1989); #305 MOTHER KNOWS BEST by
Barbara Bretton (August 1989); and #309
SAVING GRACE by Anne McAllister
(September 1989).

GULL COTTAGE—because one month can be
the start of forever...

Have You Ever Wondered If You Could Write A Harlequin Novel?

Here's great news—Harlequin is offering a series of cassette tapes to help you do just that. Written by Harlequin editors, these tapes give practical advice on how to make your characters—and your story—come alive. There's a tape for each contemporary romance series Harlequin publishes.

Mail order only

All sales final